CHASING AFTER JUSTICE

Chasing After Justice

MONTY MCKINNON

Monty McKinnon

Cover Design: Ken Steven
Author Photograph: Peter McKinnon
Stock Imagery: BigStock

ISBN: 978-1-7386509-0-3 (Paperback)
ISBN: 978-1-7386509-2-7 (eBook)
ISBN: 978-1-7386509-1-0 (Hardcover)

First Printing: 02-2023

I dedicate this book to all the wonderful people who were kind enough to answer my multitude of questions to bring this story to life with some degree of accuracy.

I am grateful for the input and encouragement of my wife, Donna, Peter McKinnon, Emily Santorelli, my EMS consultant, Matt Walton, my York Regional Police Detective, Dave Elford, and my good friend Ken Steven, who taught me so much and who encouraged me to finish this book.

All of you and so many others offered me amazing grace, knowledge, and ideas to get me thinking when I needed that the most. Thank you for your invaluable contributions because, without all of you, I don't think this book would be a reality.

Are you ready for the next one?

Chapter 1

Carson Blocker never tired of visiting the Fairmont Hotel at Banff National Park in Alberta. Gazing out one of the panoramic windows on the main floor, everywhere he looked there was one breathtaking view that was outdone by another.

It was easy to see why this area of the Canadian Rockies was heaven for photographers. Some of them were world-famous, like Peter McKinnon from the Toronto area. He captured magical moments at Mount Rundle and Moraine Lake that became immortalized on commemorative silver coins by the Royal Canadian Mint.

Another perfect postcard view could be found at Lake Louise, just an hour's drive northwest on the Trans-Canada Highway. Once you have seen its milky blue water framed by the mountains and their glaciers, the image is etched into your memory forever.

Surrounded by such beauty, Carson couldn't imagine ever living anywhere else. He was born and raised in the town of Canmore, just 20 minutes south of Banff National Park. His family owned 1,500 acres of land, a large spread with rolling hills and streams of water, ideal for grazing cattle and other livestock. It had been passed down from Carson's grandfather to Clive, his dad.

Clive was getting on in years, and while he had slowed down recently, he still liked to work the ranch. "It may be hard work," he would say, "but being outdoors in the fresh air and sunshine is my heaven on earth."

Carson and his older brother Luke knew what their father meant. They also loved the outdoors and gladly helped with chores around the ranch as they were growing up. It was easy to get things done between them, but Luke got married two years ago, and he and his wife Melissa bought their own ranch nearby. With his brother gone, it was now a full-time job for Carson to manage the day-to-day operations.

Looking across the Bow River at majestic Mount Norquay, Carson's mind began to drift as he remembered accepting the six-hour challenge to hike up the South Ridge for the first time. He suddenly felt goosebumps, and his whole body shuddered as his thoughts turned to the last time he made that trek during the winter.

Climbing Mount Norquay is not for the fearful or faint of heart. Nor are any of the other mountains in the area. Carson understood that climbing those mountains could be dangerous, especially in winter. It would be foolhardy to venture out alone. In less time than it takes to call for help, one could sustain serious injuries, broken bones, or even death. That's why he always teamed up with his best friend, Doug Anderson. The two of them were experienced climbers and sought-after hiking guides, but even experienced climbers make careless mistakes.

Recalling that day on the mountain, he and Doug were at least halfway up the South Ridge. Doug was in the lead about 10 feet in front of him. Their back-and-forth banter was all the distraction it took for disaster to unfold. Without warning, Carson's foot slipped on loose, icy gravel. He struggled to retain his balance, but the 60-pound weight of all the supplies in his backpack, not to mention a small tent and sleeping bag, was too much for him to control.

He felt himself falling backward, then tumbling like clothes in a dryer as he rolled down the rocky, snow-covered mountainside, gaining speed as he bounced from one rock to another. The sky was spinning, and snow twisted around his head as he violently hit one shoulder and then the other. He was out of control, sliding, falling, and sometimes flying through midair.

Carson's rapid descent came to a sudden stop as his body slammed into a wall of snow and light underbrush. He felt like he had just been hit by a truck. Every square inch of his body was now aching, and his head was throbbing. Snow was swirling everywhere, blinding his vision. The wind was biting his face as he wondered: "Where am I? What just happened? Did I break any bones?" He just laid there, panting, trying to relax his body so his muscles wouldn't become tense and cold. For a moment, everything went silent and dark. His mind was flooded with crazy thoughts: "Is this it? Am I going to die here, alone on this mountain? Will anyone ever find me?"

Just then, his thoughts were interrupted by a sound. Did he hear his name, or was he dreaming? He was cold and began to shiver, which reminded him that he needed to relax and collect his thoughts if he was going to survive this tumble. There, he heard it again! Doug's voice was coming through loud and clear from his two-way radio, "Carson, where are you? Carson, can you hear me? Damn it, Carson, you better be okay!"

Carson tried to move to reach his radio, and a feeling of panic overcame him when he realized both arms were pinned to his sides by the snow and underbrush. All he could do was lie there and wait.

Static transmissions continued with slight pauses, interrupting Doug's desperate voice: "Carson, can you hear me? Carson, answer me!"

As an experienced hiker, Carson knew if Doug didn't find him soon, the cold wind would intensify, and the wind chill would freeze him to death. "Hurry Doug," Carson thought. "Please hurry!"

Minutes passed that seemed like hours to Carson until he could hear his best friend bellowing in the distance: "Carson, Carson, are you okay? Carson, are you hurt? Carson, where are you? Carson, answer me! Carson, can you hear me?"

"Over here, Doug!" Carson had used every ounce of his strength to shout those few words as his body rebelled with pain.

"I've got you, Carson! Hang on, I'm coming!"

Carson was startled as a bird flew by the hotel window, breaking his momentary trance and bringing him back into a warm and comfortable room. He knew how fortunate he was that day, a day that could have turned out quite differently if it weren't for Doug. After he was airlifted from the mountain, he spent a week in the hospital suffering from a severe concussion and several cracked ribs, not to mention many cuts, scrapes, and bruises.

Carson knew he could count on Doug to always be there for him and vice versa. Being strong and athletic, they both enjoyed hiking, skiing, and hockey. But of all the sports they played, golf was their favorite, and they constantly challenged one another with small side wagers on the course. For years they had been discussing their dream of owning a golf course and becoming CPGA golf pros. That's why what happened three years ago was still so unbelievable to Carson.

He and Doug were playing their usual Saturday game of golf, but Carson could tell something was off. Doug had not been his usual talkative self during the front nine. At the time, Carson chalked it up to the fact he was beating Doug so badly. He even wondered if Doug was purposely throwing the game. When they reached the halfway house, Carson ordered a hot dog as usual, but Doug said he wasn't hungry. His face was ashen, and the faint smile on his face turned into a frown.

"What's wrong Doug?"

"Carson, I don't know how to tell you this. You're not going to like it. I'm moving to Toronto."

Carson began to tremble. "Doug, this isn't funny. What are you talking about?"

"I've accepted a job at a real estate firm in Toronto. The owner, William Nash, is a long-time friend of my father. I've gotten to know him pretty well over the past few summers that he's been vacationing at the Fairmont."

"What are you talking about, Doug? You're kidding me, right? Why would you do this?"

"I want to make money Carson. Real money. Toronto is the place to live and have it all. The real estate market is booming, and William Nash says if I come to work for him at Complete Real Estate, he'll ensure I get my real estate licence in less than a year. Nash is retiring in a few years, and he said if I prove myself, he could see me taking over the business."

"Doug, I can't believe you're doing this. What about our plans for a golf course? I thought you wanted to become a golf pro?"

"Carson, it's time for a reality check, my friend. With the pittance you make managing your dad's ranch, and the minimum wage plus tips I get as a bartender at the Fairmont, we're never going to be able to earn enough money to make that dream come true. I want money, Carson. Big money! And I want it now. Opportunity is knocking for me in Toronto. I'm answering the door."

Carson was aware he had been gazing out the window for quite some time while daydreaming and reliving the past. Twilight was approaching, and although another glorious view would usually spellbind him, he wasn't in the mood right now. His dream was dead, and he knew it.

Chapter 2

The next morning came too quickly for Carson as he lay in bed, thinking about the chores he had to get done. After a quick breakfast, he noticed the air was fresh and still as he walked toward the barn, coffee cup in hand. The early morning sunlight was casting shadows that seemed to dance as they streaked through the barn boards to the straw on the floor. He had just begun cleaning out the horse stalls when he was interrupted by the ringtone of his cell phone.

"Hey man," said Carson as he clicked on the speaker, setting his phone on a bed of hay.

"Carson, you have to come to Toronto."

"Doug, we've talked about this so many times. Why do you keep calling me and bugging me to come to Toronto? I'm perfectly happy here in Canmore."

Carson was lying, and he knew it. He had been miserable ever since his best friend had moved to Toronto. Carson missed their adventures together and their friendly rivalry on the golf course. And he was bored of the never-changing routine of managing the ranch. Not a day went by lately when he didn't think, "Surely there must be more to life than this."

"Carson, William Nash just made me a partner in the firm. Toronto is booming even more now with opportunity. There's a fortune to be made in real estate. I own several properties now, and it's amazing how much money I'm making. If you join me here at Complete Real Estate, together we could make enough money to finally build that golf course we always dreamed of. I'll take you under my wing and show you the ropes. What do you say, Carson? Pack your bags and get on the next plane to Toronto. If it turns out that you don't like it here, you can always go home. You have nothing to lose!"

"That's easy for you to say, Doug, but right now I'm up to my ankles in manure. I can't leave the ranch. My dad needs me here to look after things."

"Stop making excuses, my friend. Why not hire someone else to help? Then you'd be free to come to Toronto where you belong. Just come out here and at least look at the opportunity. I'll meet you at the airport and you can stay with me until you get settled in. What do you say?"

Chapter 3

A hand reached out from under the warm bed covers in search of the off switch to an annoyingly loud buzzer. It sounded like a firetruck driving through Carson's head, blasting its horn repeatedly. Looking over at the bedside table, he saw '5:15' pulsing in red light on his clock. Groaning, he lifted his arm and hit the snooze button with one purposeful strike. All was silent, dark, and peaceful again.

This morning, his regular exercise routine would have to wait. He was too tired, and there were too many things to do today and not enough time. Looking out the window and into the distance, he could see sunrise trying to peek through the somewhat dark and cold-looking clouds. "Sunrise here," he mused, "was nothing compared to sunrise on the ranch outside Canmore."

As he waited for his first cup of coffee to brew, he wondered how Doug had ever convinced him to move to Toronto ten years ago. Not that he was complaining. Everything Doug had promised and more had come true. It turned out that he had a natural talent for buying and selling real estate. No one could argue with the statistics.

Since he came on board, company profits had grown 30 percent a year, twice the rate of previous years. Doug had purchased Complete Real Estate from William Nash, and Carson was now his partner. He was the best man at Doug's wedding, and Doug was the best man at his. And both of their golf games were better than ever.

However, their regular Saturday game would have to wait for the next two weeks because Doug was on vacation in Hawaii with his wife, Donna. And while he was gone, Carson was in charge of the office, which is why he was so tired. Juggling his own client list and being available to review and approve the deals of all the other agents was beginning to take its toll on him.

Coffee in hand, Carson headed over to the TV and turned on the morning news.

"This is John Mackie reporting live for Canwide News on this beautiful Thursday morning. I'm at the scene of a horrific vehicle crash. Over my shoulder are the remains of an SUV whose driver lost control following a high-speed police chase. It's a miracle that only the driver is injured after the vehicle mounted a curb and plowed through some gardens, running over numerous children's toys before slamming into a 100-year-old oak tree. As you can see, the entire front end of the vehicle is destroyed, and the fire department needed to use the jaws of life to free the occupant.

"Reliable sources have told us that the driver of this SUV did not have a driver's licence because he is only fifteen years old. The good news is the young man was not seriously injured. Without a doubt, a seat belt and airbags saved his life today. This time, the fifteen-year-old was very lucky. This is John Mackie reporting live for Canwide News from the scene of yet another police car chase gone wrong."

Chapter 4

Neighbors who had seldom seen one another during the long cold winter months were now all standing on their front porches looking in amazement at the sight before them.

Red and blue flashing police car lights made for an eerie scene while steam hissed from a crumpled SUV, wafting into the air before mingling with the few clouds in the sky. Yellow police tape surrounded the area, and several police constables were busy taking photographs of what remained of the SUV and damage to the surrounding property.

Police Constable Gibson had just finished restraining the underage driver of the vehicle in handcuffs. Looking over his shoulder, the young man noticed the Can-wide News crew on the scene. "This is so awesome," he thought, "I'm going to be famous."

With his live report finished, John Mackie replaced the grimace on his face with a genuine smile while lowering and disconnecting his microphone. It was an early start to the day, even for a reporter who was always on the lookout for the next big news story. Maybe his next broadcast would feature a dead body or two. That might be just what he needed to increase his ratings and perhaps see him promoted to a national news spot.

The handcuffed boy glanced at the front of the vehicle he had been driving. On the lawn, he could see a small bicycle lying on its side with its front wheel intact, but the back wheel crumpled into a heap of twisted, broken metal. He marveled at the tire ruts he had created on the otherwise well-manicured lawn.

He knew his friends would be jealous seeing him featured on the television news shows today, detailing the destruction he had caused. He would be a hero to his friends, and this should qualify him for membership in his street gang of choice.

A member of the Emergency Medical Services team had already examined the boy and bandaged a few superficial cuts. "There are no serious injuries here, Constable Gibson, so we'll be leaving. The young man is in good shape, so he's cleared to travel to the station for questioning. Here's a copy of our paperwork."

Constable Gibson maneuvered the juvenile driver into the back of his cruiser and headed for the police station.

Meanwhile, Detective Sergeant Mark Borden, a twenty-five-year veteran of the Toronto Police Service, had walked into his favorite diner and sauntered to his usual booth in the back corner of the restaurant.

As the regular patrons were leaving, they walked back to greet Borden at his table. Most felt sorry for him; at least, they thought they should.

Emily approached Borden's table with a newspaper and a hot pot of coffee. Turning over the green mug on the table, she began to fill it. She liked Borden and had been bringing breakfast to him ever since he started coming to the restaurant.

"Good morning, Mark. Have you decided what you would like for breakfast?"

She didn't know that only family members called him by his first name. Everyone else called him Borden. He didn't like anyone trying to get close to him by using his first name. But Emily, in a way, was like family.

"How about some sausage and two eggs, toast, and jam, Emily?"

"Coming right up. Here's today's paper for you."

Between sips of coffee, Borden buried his head into the newspaper, starting with the front page before moving straight to the sports section.

He set down the paper, then reached for his cell phone and started scrolling through photos of his family. He stopped when he landed on the last one, which he had taken of his son, Mark Jr.

Borden was still tormented by the death of his son three years ago from a drug overdose. Mark Jr. was only 16 years old with so much to live for. Borden thought he had done everything he could to help his son get clean and sober. He had paid for extensive treatment and even enrolled him in a residential drug and alcohol rehabilitation program in Ottawa.

He still vividly remembered the final meeting with the doctors and counselors before bringing his son back home. They assured him that Mark Jr. had made excellent progress and was ready to be released.

Borden knew from his work as a cop that drugs were a curse that affected many families and ruined so many lives. "But not this time," Borden had reflected. "We have another chance to get junior's life turned around, and we're going to do it."

That night, he remembered watching the game between the Blue Jays and the Yankees. The game was halted twice by rain in New York. When the game ended in victory for the Blue Jays, Borden walked upstairs to get ready for bed. As he passed Mark Jr.'s door, he knocked softly and peeked inside. Mark was sleeping quietly with a peaceful look on his face. "It doesn't matter how old your children are," Borden thought, "they always look like angels while they sleep."

The next morning arrived with the sun streaming through Borden's bedroom window. It was a Friday. Before heading out to work, he knocked on the door to his son's room to say goodbye. Mark Jr. didn't answer. He called out to him, and still no answer or movement from the room. Entering his son's bedroom, Borden saw a still, ghostly white, and breathless body, and knew that Mark Jr. was gone. He sat on the edge of the bed and cried as only a parent who had lost a loved one could understand.

He missed Mark Jr. so much that he wondered if he would ever recover. Therapy from a psychologist had helped him, but not to the extent that he and his wife Lois had hoped. Lois seemed to have made better progress than him. They stuck together, helping each other, listening to each other, and sometimes crying together.

At the urging of his psychologist, Borden sought closure, so he began working closely with a team of constables focused on removing drugs from the streets of Toronto. He joined them on drug raids and chased after justice by working the drug beat in his spare time.

Borden financially supported charities focused on helping young adults and teens struggling with drug issues. He spoke to students and parents, warning them about the devastating dangers of drugs. All he wanted to do was turn his personal tragedy into a win for some other person or their family.

As he closed the photo app on his cell phone, Borden noticed it was 7:45. It was time to get to work. He paid his bill, leaving a generous tip for Emily, and headed out the door to make the short drive to his office.

Approaching the police station, Borden noticed a uniformed constable ahead of him. He quickly realized it was Ted Gibson, skillfully moving an obvious delinquent toward the station entrance.

Constable Gibson was a recent recruit from the police academy with a promising future in law enforcement. He had graduated with honors, and everyone at the station enjoyed having him as a colleague.

The teenager had blood on his face, disheveled hair, and scrawny weak-looking arms handcuffed behind him. He was poorly dressed in tattered clothes, which exuded an odor beyond description.

His foul mouth was moving a mile a minute, spewing obscenities, but his belligerent attitude didn't seem to faze Gibson, who demonstrated great restraint.

Catching up to Gibson, Borden asked, "What's up with this?"

Gibson replied without skipping a beat, "He's the individual who was seen stealing an SUV from a downtown auto dealer. The citizen who witnessed the crime called 911."

"Is this the high-speed pursuit in a residential area I heard about on the television early this morning?"

"Yes sir, we got the call and just happened to be in the area. In no time, we caught up to him. He was driving recklessly, swerving from one side of the road to the other at high speed, when we began following him.

"We took a dashcam video, as we were in pursuit. When he was speeding through the residential area, he lost control of the vehicle. During the chase, he managed to sideswipe one car and just missed two other parked vehicles before he mounted a curb, narrowly missing some joggers on the sidewalk, who were out for an early morning run."

Borden wasn't looking for a play-by-play of Gibson's experience, as he looked at his watch.

"When we questioned him at the scene," Gibson continued, "he told us that stealing the SUV was part of an initiation, where recruits had to demonstrate their willingness to break the law to gain entry and acceptance into their gang."

"So, Gibson," Borden asked as the young constable took a breath, "do you think drugs were involved in this situation?"

"We found drugs in his possession, and he appears to be high. The timestamp shows he was also texting while we were chasing him, which explains his erratic driving. There was a gun in the driver's-side door pocket. It was loaded and ready for use. We bagged it and will check for fingerprints and examine it to determine if it was fired recently or used in any other crimes."

"Wonderful," thought Borden, "now this kid will have a criminal record just so he can belong to a gang that's going nowhere. What's wrong with some young people? They have every opportunity to do something successful with their lives and waste it instead."

"Did you explain his rights to him, Gibson?"

"Yes sir, I did."

"Good. Be sure to drop off your paperwork to Detective Cross when it is completed."

"Yes sir, I will."

As the three men entered the building, Constable Gibson directed his foul-smelling suspect toward the holding cells away from, and thankfully downwind, from Borden.

Borden strode down to the detectives' office area, a large, open room crowded with multiple desks and chairs. Dozens of visitors and personnel were moving about with seemingly disorganized activity. He offered short, friendly greetings to fellow detectives as he headed toward his office.

Borden's office was not large, but it was tidy. With multiple pictures of his family, including Mark Jr., on the wall and on the credenza behind his desk, it felt homey, which seemed appropriate since he usually spent more time in the office than at his house.

There were letters of praise from the Chief of Police hanging on one wall and a commendation from the Mayor's Office, along with a certificate honoring his 25 years of service on the force.

A large, wooden-framed window directly opposite his desk allowed him an unobstructed view of the general office to monitor what was or was not happening with his staff of detectives. Looking through that window now, he could see Detective Cross entering the office area.

As a former instructor at the Police Academy, Janet Cross knew how to handle herself in difficult situations. She was proficient in the use of tactical weapons and excelled at hand-to-hand combat. Her successful record of arrests had allowed her to move up quickly through the ranks. Despite her toughness, she could also be gentle, thoughtful, and kind-hearted toward her colleagues and departmental staff.

Cross picked up a file folder from her desk and tucked it under her arm. Then with a coffee in one hand and a muffin in the other, she quickly marched over to detective Borden's office for their regular morning briefing session.

Cross admired Detective Borden and was pleased to be working alongside him. Even though she had been an instructor at the Police Academy, she knew she could still learn plenty from him. Being able to tap into Borden's 25 years of field experience was a huge benefit.

Handing her folder to Borden, Cross said, "Not much going on, boss. I think it will be a quiet day."

"I certainly hope so, Cross. We have more than enough work to do around here as it is. What are you working on?"

"I just interviewed John Barber, owner of a local hardware store that was robbed three nights ago."

"So, how's that going?"

"Slow. Not much to go on. No witnesses, no video, and no money was taken. A few handguns are missing and two rifles, along with some ammo. No doubt they will end up in the wrong hands, and that's worrisome."

Borden nodded in agreement. "Keep digging. I'm confident you'll find something. Anything else I should know about?"

"Constable Gibson just handed me the paperwork on a young man he arrested this morning for stealing an

SUV from a car dealership in what appears to be some kind of gang-related initiation."

"Yes, I saw Gibson as he was bringing the kid in."

"I'm heading down the hall to interrogate the suspect now, boss. I'll let you know what I find out."

Chapter 5

Carson and his assistant Andrea Talbot had spent the entire afternoon and a good part of the evening sorting through a massive list of properties within a two-hour drive from the office. They were creating a shortlist to show William and Sara Porter, two old friends of his from Canmore. Carson knew the Porters had their hearts set on buying a small hobby farm or a property with some acreage. He wanted to impress them with some amazing listings.

"Andrea, were you able to reserve dinner for me and the Porters at my golf club tomorrow night? It would be the perfect place for us to relax and catch up after a full day of touring."

"Yes, everything is all set. They assured me that you'll have your favorite table with a panoramic view of the golf course."

Carson felt a little excited about the day ahead as he longed to connect with familiar faces from back home and, at the same time, have them see how successful he had become since his move to Toronto.

"That's perfect. I think we're ready for tomorrow. Let's call it a night, Andrea. Thanks for working late. Let me walk you out."

"Carson, aren't you leaving now too?"

"No, not right now. Since I'll be out of the office all day tomorrow, I think it's best if I tackle the mountain of paperwork that's piled up on my desk with Doug being away. I really don't want to worry about paperwork when I'm trying to close a sale with the Porters."

As Andrea headed to her car, Carson locked the office door and turned off the general office lighting since all the other agents and office staff had left hours ago.

Feeling a bit tired, Carson yawned and strolled down to the kitchen to make a fresh pot of coffee to fuel his late-night work session. While he waited for it to brew, he sauntered back to his office to examine the stack of files he needed to get through.

Noticing his golf putter leaned against the wall, Carson couldn't resist the distraction. He rolled his first putt dead center in the automated cup that spit back his ball along the smooth carpet. He welcomed a few minutes to practice his putting because golf is what grounded him. And besides that, anything he could do to beat Doug in their first match after he returned from Hawaii was time well spent.

Carson's concentration was broken by the aroma of freshly brewed coffee that awaited him. That smell and the first sip of fresh coffee energized his entire body.

With a large cup in hand, he returned to the pile of paperwork he could no longer avoid.

Reviewing the deals that agents submit for approval was time-consuming and tedious, but it needed to be done. Scrutinizing these files gave Carson a newfound appreciation of the extra work that Doug needed to do as the owner of Complete Real Estate. "Thank goodness I will only have to do this for one more week," he thought.

After finishing off the last coffee from the pot he brewed earlier, Carson pushed himself back from his desk and stood up to stretch. Inspecting his new Rolex, he noticed that the paperwork took much longer than he had expected. It was almost 3:00 in the morning! He needed to get home and get at least a couple of hours of shuteye and freshen up to get back here for his meeting with the Porters. Chuckling to himself, Carson thought he better make a pit stop to get rid of all the coffee he'd been drinking before he headed out.

Returning to his office from the washroom a few minutes later, Carson was startled to see an intruder dressed in black and wearing a black ski mask concealing his face. The thief was a few inches shorter than Carson's six-foot height and skinny as a bean pole. He had already disconnected Carson's laptop from the power supply and closed it up to take with him.

"Who the hell are you and what are you doing here?" yelled Carson. "Put that computer down. I'm calling the cops."

In a panic, the intruder grabbed a paperweight from the desk and hurled it at him. Carson ducked just in time as the paperweight whizzed past his right ear.

With his adrenaline spiking, Carson darted toward the intruder and grabbed hold of him before he could scurry around the desk and head toward the door.

The thief threw a punch that hit Carson square on his jaw.

Being a sturdy man, having grown up on the ranch, Carson had no problem flinging his skinny opponent across his desk to the floor on the other side. The paperwork he had so painstakingly completed went flying everywhere around the room.

Scampering back to his feet, the intruder scanned the room for anything he could use as a weapon. He reached over and grabbed the golf putter he saw leaning against the wall by the desk and swung it wildly at Carson, hitting him solidly on his left ribcage.

Carson staggered and gasped for air as he felt the sharp, jabbing pain like a blow from a hammer.

With adrenaline masking his pain, Carson frantically looked for a weapon he could use. He grabbed his prized golf trophy from the bookshelf and raised it above his head to inflict a forceful blow as he lunged toward his assailant.

Less than a second later, he was stopped dead in his tracks by a deafening sound and a fiery pain in his right shoulder. The trophy he was wielding fell to the floor. Just then, his assailant pushed Carson out of the way with all his scrawny might as he ran toward the office door.

The searing pain intensified as Carson was hurled backward. He stumbled over a box of files on the floor and smashed his head on the edge of his desk before collapsing into unconsciousness.

The masked intruder, shaking with fear and panting for breath, glanced back to see Carson lying motionless on the floor beside his desk.

The deathly silence was interrupted by another voice yelling at him, "Grab the laptop and let's get out of here." As he reached for the laptop, his accomplice walked over to Carson's body and grabbed his wallet from his pocket. Blood was trickling slowly from the gunshot wound and pooling on the carpet.

The two intruders quickly snatched more laptops from neighboring offices on the way down the hall toward the exit leading to the underground parking garage. They hustled to their SUV, parked right across from the exit door. For a moment, the two of them just sat there in silence, panting as they tried to catch their breath. They both scanned the garage with intensity and, not seeing anyone, removed their masks.

"I can't believe there was still someone in the office at this hour. How did we miss seeing that, Derek? We took every precaution to be sure that nobody was around."

"Why did you have to shoot him Stan? What if he dies?"

"Hey little brother, it was a split-second decision. It was either him or you. He was two seconds away from splitting your head open with that golf trophy. I didn't have a choice."

"Thanks. But you know Madler is going to be pissed when he hears what happened and that the real estate guy was shot. I'm scared. What will happen if he dies? The cops will start a major manhunt looking for us and it will be all over the news. How will we get away?"

"Let's worry about that later. I'll take care of Madler. Right now, we need to drive away as if nothing happened. The last thing we need is to attract attention, so be careful how you drive. Let's go straight to our safe house and set things up there in case we have to move on."

A moment later, the SUV casually wound its way through the underground garage and up the exit ramp, turned right onto the deserted street, and headed north into the night.

Chapter 6

Noticing Borden was ready to go, Emily quickly brought his bill to the table. "Was today's breakfast one that will make you miss our cooking while you're away on vacation, Mark?"

Borden chuckled, "Absolutely Emily. If this were my last meal, I'd die a happy man. Please give my compliments to the chef."

He was hoping this was going to be a slow day. The plan was for him to leave work early and get home to pack for the start of his annual four-week vacation. It had been postponed twice already because of an unexpected workload, something that did not sit well with his wife, Lois.

He and Lois were looking forward to spending time at their cabin with their son and daughter, who were both home from college and would be joining them. It was Borden's chance to unwind and forget all about his stressful and sometimes terrifying job. One whole month with no phone calls, no emergencies, no meetings, and no demands on his time other than firing up the BBQ.

Arriving at the station just in time for his regular 8:00 briefing with Cross, he walked briskly to his corner office. No time for friendly chit-chat with his fellow detectives today. He was on a mission to wrap things up quickly and head home. Seeing that Cross was already at her desk, he waved at her to join him in his office.

"Good morning, Cross. Please tell me that crime has finally taken a holiday in this city so that I can finally take mine."

With a big smile, she happily responded, "Today is your lucky day, boss! Since my debrief on events yesterday, things have been very quiet. There's nothing worth mentioning at this point."

"You're next in line for promotion to Detective Sergeant. That's why I asked you to be in charge of the other detectives while I'm away, and to handle whatever comes up. Are you still okay with that?"

"No problem, Borden. I'll look after everything while you're gone. I hope you have a great holiday. You certainly deserve it. Is there anything else?"

"Not right now, but if something comes up, I'll let you know before I leave. Consider yourself in charge as of now."

Cross returned to her desk with a grin on her face. She welcomed the opportunity to practice being the boss of the department. And she wouldn't be happy until she broke the glass ceiling to become the first female Chief of Police.

Borden picked up the phone to call his administrative assistant, "Caroline, can you call the prosecutor and confirm the time of our luncheon appointment today and where we're meeting? Please let him know I must be back here at 2:00 for a meeting with the Chief."

Before Caroline could answer, a loud commotion broke out in the outer office. Looking through the glass window of his office, Borden saw Detectives Kim and Friedman scurrying around, reaching for their vests, shoulder holsters, and jackets. He wanted to step in but remembered Cross was now in charge.

Just then, there was a loud knock on the door, and before he could say anything, Cross came barging in. "I know you're planning on leaving soon, but I thought you'd like to know what has just happened. There has been a shooting."

"What the hell," exclaimed Borden. "Where, when, what happened? Was anyone hurt?"

"One person was reportedly shot. EMS is on the way there. The shooting happened at a real estate firm in North York."

"Are you kidding me?" asked Borden. "A real estate firm? Why would anyone shoot at a real estate office? Did someone pay too much for a house? Grab your gear. We need to check this out."

Caroline was now standing outside his door. "Caroline, call the prosecutor's office and cancel my luncheon, and notify the Chief that I may not be at the Department Heads meeting."

He grabbed his vest and reached into a secure cabinet beside his desk for his gun and ammunition.

"Cross, are you ready?" hollered Borden.

"Yes sir," responded Cross.

"Let's roll. You drive."

Chapter 7

Arriving at the office just before 8:00, Andrea parked in her usual spot out front. Delicately balancing a big box of pastries she had picked up on the way, she fumbled inside her handbag and fished out the key to open the front door. The office didn't open until 9:00, so she would have plenty of time to set things up in the boardroom for Carson's presentation to William and Sara Porter.

Stepping inside, Andrea flicked on the general office lighting and made her way down to the kitchen. Placing the box of pastries on the counter, she began preparing the coffee machine to brew a fresh pot. Then she laid out an assortment of pastries on a serving tray and carried it down to the boardroom.

After taking a few minutes to make sure the room was neat and tidy, Andrea headed down another hallway toward Carson's office to pick up the files they had prepared the night before.

Just outside the doorway to his office, she noticed something on the floor. As she got closer, she recognized that it was the paperweight Carson always kept on his desk. "That's odd," she thought. "Why would this be here?"

Andrea bent down to pick it up and sauntered into Carson's office. She gasped as she saw files and papers strewn across the floor. Then her eyes fixed on Carson's legs protruding from behind his desk.

For a moment, Andrea was paralyzed with fear. Then she screamed, "Carson! Carson, are you okay?" But Carson did not move.

Dashing to her office, Andrea called 911, trembling uncontrollably as she waited for someone to answer.

"This is 911. What is the nature of your emergency?"

"I just got to the office and my boss is lying on the floor and there's blood on the carpet and he's not moving."

"Is he breathing?"

"I don't know, but his office is a mess. He's not moving. It looks like there was a fight. Files and papers are all over the floor."

"Could you please give me your name?"

"My name is Andrea Talbot."

"Andrea, is anybody else in the office hurt?"

"I'm the only one here and my boss is not moving. Please send someone. He needs help,"

"Is the door to the office building open?"

"Yes, it's open."

"I have just dispatched the local EMS, and the police are on their way."

"Please tell them to hurry!"

"They should be arriving within the next five minutes. In the meantime, Andrea, please stay on the line with me."

The next few minutes seemed like an eternity to Andrea. The first police on the scene were Constable Gibson and his partner Constable Grant. Andrea frantically led them down a hallway to Carson's office.

Gibson attempted to locate a pulse in Carson's neck and then glanced back at his partner. "He's still alive. Looks like he's been shot. This is now a crime scene. We need to lock this place down. I'll stand by the front door to keep everyone out until our backup and EMS arrives. Take pictures of the body. Then call in the situation here immediately and console Ms. Talbot until the detectives can get here."

Approaching the front door, Gibson was greeted by flashing lights and the sound of sirens. Two more police cruisers, followed closely by an ambulance, came racing down the street and turned into the parking lot out front.

While the EMS team unloaded their gear, Gibson sent his backup team into action. "The office opens in less than half an hour. Staff and customers will begin arriving soon. Secure the perimeter, including the entrance and exit to the parking garage. Nobody is allowed in or out except the detectives and forensics."

By now, the fire department had also arrived on the scene and rushed to help the ambulance team carry their gear and gurney through the front door. Gibson ushered them all down to Carson's office.

With speed and precision, the EMS team approached the motionless body lying on the carpeted floor. They dropped their kit bags, unzipped them, and got to work.

One paramedic quickly covered the gunshot wound to Carson's upper right shoulder. "The gunshot wound is not serious. It must have missed any major arteries because the blood has already clotted."

Another paramedic bandaged the gash on Carson's head that had also congealed. "Constable Gibson, judging by the length of time it takes blood to clot, this man sustained these injuries several hours ago. If he doesn't regain consciousness soon, there will be a risk of serious brain damage. There is not a minute to spare."

"Understood, He's all yours. We've already taken some pictures."

As the ambulance team carefully lifted Carson onto their gurney, Gibson turned his attention to the paramedic from the fire department. "The woman who found him is with my partner right now, and she seemed to be in shock. Before you leave, can you check in on her to make sure she is alright?"

Contacting his partner via their two-way radio, Gibson discovered he and Andrea were in the kitchen. As they entered the room, Andrea was babbling incoherently.

Chapter 8

Borden and Cross arrived at the shooting scene as the paramedics were lifting Carson into the ambulance. Borden moved directly toward one of the paramedics asking, "How's your patient?"

"He's alive but still unconscious, so we need to get him to the hospital quickly, detective. You can question him there."

"Will do. Thanks."

Borden and Cross entered the office, where they were greeted by Constable Gibson. "Detective Borden! I wasn't expecting to see you here today. Aren't you supposed to be going on holiday?"

"Not until this day is over, Gibson. Let's see if we can wrap this up soon. What do you have for us?"

"Sir, the administrative assistant told me the shooting victim, Carson Blocker, was working late. Someone broke into the office via the door from the underground parking garage. There are signs of a struggle taking place. At some point the victim was shot in the shoulder from behind, possibly hitting his head as he fell to the floor.

He was still unconscious when we arrived. Follow me detectives and I'll take you to the office."

Stepping inside Carson's office, both Borden and Cross silently scanned the scene.

"Where was the victim found, Gibson?" asked Borden.

"Right here, sir. Constable Grant took these photos and uploaded them to the Forensic Team."

"Cross, look at these photos. Something is not right here."

"Why do you say that?"

"Glancing over the room, I see a golf putter, a trophy, and a bunch of files on the floor, which indicates that a struggle took place here. I don't think it is likely that the victim would've turned his back on the intruder if they were having a fight. The location of the victim's body makes me wonder if there could be a second person who entered the office during the scuffle and was the actual shooter."

"Yes Borden! It's very plausible that's what happened. We'll know more once we get an opportunity to question the victim at the hospital."

Borden nodded in agreement. "We need to speak with his administrative assistant now. Maybe she can confirm my theory about what transpired here. Gibson, did you say she was in the kitchen?"

Yes, sir. I'll take you and Detective Cross there now. Her name is Andrea Talbot. She seems quite hysterical, and I have a fire department paramedic attending to her right now."

Entering the kitchen, they found the paramedic kneeling beside Andrea and busily checking her vital signs. "I gave her a mild sedative to help calm her. She's in shock, so I've called for another ambulance to take her to the hospital for observation."

Andrea was sitting, elbows on her knees, with her face buried in her hands.

"Andrea, do you mind if I call you Andrea?"

"That's fine."

"Andrea, I'm Detective Borden, and this is Detective Cross. Could we speak with you for a moment?"

Andrea nodded her agreement.

"You told Constable Gibson you didn't see the shooting, but could you give us an overview of your day leading up to finding the body in the office this morning?"

Andrea began to fidget in her seat and struggled to breathe as she recounted her activities.

"I think I drove...yes, I drove my daughter and dropped her off at her school.

"I think I took her to school...yes, I took her to get pastries.

"Is my daughter home from school?

"She wants a dog, you know...I told her one day she could have a dog.

"I went to a bakery and bought some pastries for Mr. Blocker and his clients.

"He likes fresh pastries and coffee, you know.

"I love my daughter...I should buy her a dog.

"He will be here soon to meet with his clients...they are friends of his."

Shaking and crying, Andrea kept mumbling incoherently.

"Why would... to hurt Mr. Blocker?

"Is my daughter home from school?"

The paramedic looked up at Borden. "I'm sorry, Detective, Andrea is in no shape to continue. She's verging on hysteria."

"Okay then, you should go. We'll catch up at the hospital."

The paramedic escorted Andrea to the front door, where the waiting EMS team placed her on a gurney and wheeled her out to their waiting ambulance.

Borden and Cross checked in with the Forensic Team, who were busy taking photos, dusting for fingerprints, taking blood samples, and collecting fibers in Carson's office. So far, there was not much to indicate who else might have been involved in this incident.

"Cross, while the Forensic Team is finishing up here, we need to determine if this was just a shooting or a robbery gone wrong. I noticed a lot of the office staff have arrived for work and are huddled in the parking lot, wondering what's happening. Round up Detectives Kim and Friedman, and let's start questioning them. With a bit of luck, one of them might give us a clue to what happened here last night."

Chapter 9

The 26-foot inboard mahogany wood boat glided into one of the three slips in a stunning log-framed boat-house. Turning off the engine, Carlos Martinez threw rubber bumpers over both sides and securely tied the launch to the dock anchors. Tapping the switch for the electric opener, he watched as the lakefront door of the boathouse closed quietly behind him.

Halfway up the fieldstone path to the front veranda of his majestic six-bedroom log home, he suddenly became mindful of the peace and serenity that surrounded him. It was a sharp contrast to the hustle and bustle that was so much a part of his daily life working in Ottawa, the nation's capital.

Martinez plopped himself on a puffy outdoor sofa on the veranda of what he called 'the cottage.' From his seat, he had a panoramic view of Lake Muskoka. This secluded location on his own private island, he thought, was a perfect place for a meeting that needed to remain private.

Today he would be welcoming Miguel Valdez, the CEO of a thriving Mexican railway, and Juan Estrada, the man they both had hand-picked to head up the Canadian distribution operation. If all went well in the next few hours, business could soon be booming for everyone concerned.

The peace and tranquility of the moment were suddenly broken by the distinct ringtone of a burner phone. "Your timing couldn't be worse, Mr. Madler. I'm expecting our guests from Mexico to arrive any minute now."

"I'm sorry to bother you Señor Martinez, but there's been a development that I thought you should know about. Two of my men last night were interrupted by an employee during an after-hours visit to a real estate office. They were able to obtain the information we were looking for, but the employee was shot during a scuffle. The police are still conducting their investigation at the scene."

"Will anyone be able to identify your men?"

"Not a chance. They disabled the video security system before entering the building, and they both wore masks. They're laying low at the safe house now and I've just sent a few men over with a care package to set things up in case they need to make a hasty exit."

"I'm sure you realize that the last thing we all need right now is a massive screw up, Mr. Madler. I trust you will keep this situation under control."

As Martinez terminated the call and tucked the burner phone back into his pocket, he could hear the drone of a helicopter in the distance. Glancing out over the calm waters of the lake, he watched the dot on the horizon grow bigger as it approached. He got up and made his way down to the helipad beside the boathouse.

The helicopter blades stirred up the water as it slowly descended onto the landing pad. The door opened, and two men stepped out, crouching beneath the blades that were still slowly swirling as they made their way to greet their host.

Martinez ushered his two guests to the veranda, where they watched in silence as the helicopter lifted off and headed back to the mainland for refueling.

After pouring his guests coffee and offering them some pastry treats, Martinez turned to Valdez and asked when the pilot would return.

"He'll be back at noon."

"That's perfect. Let's get down to business. Señor Valdez, when we were together in Mexico, you indicated to me that you had a variety of products that you wanted to distribute here in Canada."

"Yes, that is correct. Juan is the one who will oversee the acquisition and movement of products from Mexico to Canada. Right now, my struggle is having more product than buyers, so I need new distribution centers here, and the sooner the better."

Martinez smiled, knowing that he had the solution for Valdez. "My associate, Jason Madler, is a wizard when it comes to real estate. He has established distribution capabilities through the acquisition of warehouses in every major Canadian city. We've also been able to hire a number of Mexican citizens living here in Canada to work in each of those facilities. They have all been carefully vetted and can be trusted."

Juan had been listening intently. "Señor Martinez, has the final test shipment we sent been received at the Toronto warehouse yet?"

"Yes, the railcars sent by Señor Valdez arrived right on schedule. I must say, it is brilliant how you manage to keep the trains all running on time."

"Have the workers in the warehouse started repackaging the product for local distribution?"

"Yes, Juan. They started first thing this morning. As soon as the helicopter returns you and Señor Valdez to Toronto, I would like you to go straight to the warehouse to begin supervising the operation. Mr. Madler will be there to greet you and get you up to speed on everything you'll need to know. Assuming you encounter no problems processing this test order, I see no reason why we can't immediately begin scaling to meet market demand."

Chapter 10

Borden had stopped at a red light, thinking he should have turned on the siren. "What's your take on what we know so far, Cross?"

"The evidence at the scene suggests that this was pre-planned. Whoever entered that office had done their homework. They knew where all the security cameras were and disabled them. The feed went dead at about 3:00 a.m. so we can assume that the break-in happened shortly after that. They also knew there was a back entrance to the office from the underground parking garage where they could pick the lock to gain entry without being seen."

"What we're still missing here is motive. The whole thing makes little sense to me. By all accounts, the only things missing from the real estate office are some laptop computers. Why steal only a few computers and not all the computers? And why would Carson Blocker need to be shot?"

"Borden, that's exactly what I was thinking. If this was intended to be a robbery, the thief or thieves would have commanded Mr. Blocker to put his hands in the air, take his wallet, a computer, or whatever and leave. There was no sensible reason to shoot him. And, if it was a robbery, why didn't they take his Rolex. It could easily be pawned for thousands of dollars?"

"Maybe it wasn't a robbery, Cross. Maybe Carson Blocker was targeted. When we get back to the station, run a complete background check on him and see if anything looks suspicious. Meet with the other detectives who were at the scene and compare notes to see if anyone they interviewed suggested Carson Blocker had enemies. Perhaps it was an unhappy client that came back for revenge."

"There's the entrance to the hospital parking lot, Borden. Let's hope Carson or Andrea are able to answer some of these questions for us."

Borden and Cross entered the building and headed straight to the emergency department. They were surprised at how busy it was at this hour. The waiting room was overflowing. Several children were crying while their parents tried their best to comfort them. One man had a leg supported by two boards and was writhing in pain. Another was clutching his stomach and kept hollering for a nurse. Doctors walked briskly back and forth, and nurses handed clipboards to staff while answering phones that never stopped ringing.

The two detectives walked the length of the waiting room and approached the front desk. Flashing his badge at a totally disinterested receptionist, Borden asked, "Where is Carson Blocker? How is he doing?"

"I don't have any idea who Carson Blocker is, or if he is even here. Sorry, I can't help you," replied the receptionist as she turned and picked up a folder to hand to a nurse.

"This is going to be a long day," Borden sighed as he glanced at Cross. Turning his attention back to the receptionist, in a voice that didn't disguise his agitation, he announced, "This is a police matter. Is there someone in charge here to answer my questions?"

"Maddie," the receptionist yelled. "Maddie, there are some police constables here with some questions." From out of the chaos strode a nurse whose regal bearing clearly indicated that this was her domain.

"How can I help you constables?" she asked, even before she reached them.

Borden answered, "A shooting victim was brought in here about three hours ago, and I need to check on his status. The name is Carson Blocker."

The nurse took a minute to access information on a digital tablet that she was carrying. "Mr. Blocker is in surgery and will soon be in the recovery room. Then he'll be transferred to a regular room. Is there anything else I can help you with, constables?"

Borden wanted to correct the nurse: "We aren't constables. We are detectives," but he had no time to be nitpicky today.

"Yes..." Borden looked at the name pin on the nurse's uniform, "Nurse Bixby, you could help us with another matter. Could you tell me where Andrea Talbot is? She would have arrived in an ambulance shortly after Carson Blocker from the same shooting scene at Complete Real Estate earlier today."

Again, Nurse Bixby's eyes darted to her digital tablet. "No, we don't have anyone here in the hospital with that name."

"There must be some mistake. We witnessed Andrea leaving the scene in an ambulance. She wasn't shot but was suffering from mental distress."

"No," Nurse Bixby replied. "We only received one person from the shooting and that was Mr. Carson Blocker,"

"Are you certain that another ambulance didn't arrive here after Carson Blocker? Andrea is the assistant of Carson Blocker."

Nurse Bixby was getting agitated. She knew she had to cooperate with the police, but this was her Emergency Department, and she had more important matters to tend to than playing twenty questions.

"Yes, I'm certain. No one by the name of Andrea Talbot has entered the doors of this hospital as a patient!"

Nurse Bixby began walking away.

"Just one more quick question, Nurse Bixby. Could the EMS vehicle have gone to another hospital in the area?"

"No, that's impossible," she replied, shaking her head to make sure Borden got the message.

"Why are you so certain of that?" Borden shot back.

With a sarcastic grin, Nurse Bixby replied more calmly than she felt, "Because there are no other hospitals in the area."

Borden looked at Cross. "Something's wrong with this picture. Where is that ambulance with Andrea Talbot? It should have arrived here long before we did!"

Chapter 11

The rain was pelting in puddles along the dimly lit road, deep in the back countryside of Alberta farmlands. Ominous sheets of lightning began flashing more frequently as the thunder grew louder and lasted longer. The flashes of lightning continued to brighten up the black sky, illuminating everything for a quick second, like bursting fireworks, followed by darkness again.

Luke was so familiar with this road that he could drive it half asleep. But today, it needed his full attention as he battled to hold his rusty old pickup truck steady in the gusty winds. He strained to see the view ahead, but the windshield wipers were not fast enough to clear the downpour that was now pounding his truck.

He worried that the old cedar shingles on his ranch house would be no match for this storm. The roof was something he should have repaired long ago, but with Carson now living in Toronto, the burden of caring for his parent's ranch fell solely on his shoulders. It seemed there was never enough time to take care of his own place, something that didn't please Melissa.

Melissa looked out the window just in time to see her husband's truck pulling up in front of the steps. Opening the weathered screen door, she came barreling out from the house and onto the veranda.

"Luke, bring the groceries quickly before you get soaked. This storm is going to get worse. Hurry, Luke!"

Luke scampered from the driver's seat and handed Melissa two bags of groceries. He grabbed two more and made a dash for the door.

Luke shouted to Melissa to make himself heard over the howling wind and banging shutters, "Did we lose power?"

"What?" she yelled.

"Did we lose power? The lights are out!"

The silence and stillness between each heavy clap of thunder were surreal, but the silence didn't last exceptionally long. Coming closer to Luke, she yelled, "The power went out about an hour ago."

"I'm going to go start the generator, Mel. At least we'll have the power to make supper and keep the refrigerator working."

As Luke ran down the steps, raindrops were now falling like a waterfall. With each step, the biting force of the rain and small hail stones felt like little daggers hitting his face.

Making his way to the side of the house, Luke reached the generator perched on a small cement platform to keep the groundwater away. Pulling the cover off with the wind threatening to topple him, he pulled the generator cord. Nothing happened.

"What's wrong? I just bought this thing. Come on, start!" he yelled into the wind, a wind so strong he couldn't hear his voice. He pulled the cord repeatedly. "Come on, start!"

Then he realized he had forgotten to prime the fuel line. "That's how accidents happen," he thought. He primed the fuel line and pulled the cord one more time. Instantly, the machine sprang to life, and Luke could see that the lights inside the house were dim but restored.

Looking back toward a side window, Luke saw Mel motioning for him to go back out front. Struggling to run around the corner of the house, he could see the barn door slamming open and shut in the wind.

Some of the horses had gotten out and were standing in the field but had found shelter in a field hut to keep out of the blistering rain, hail, and wind. "Those horses are smarter than me," thought Luke as he made a mad dash for the barn, slipping and sliding in some mud puddles.

He stumbled into the barn, soaked to the skin and feeling exhausted. The horses inside were stirring but seemed to understand the temper tantrum that Mother Nature was having.

Stepping back out into the rain, Luke wrestled with the wind for almost a minute before he could close and secure the door.

With the dark sky and walls of water that pummeled him as he hastened back to the house, Luke could barely make out the terrain in front of him, even though he had walked this way a thousand times. Catching his foot on a tree root, he tumbled to the ground. A searing pain shot through his leg, just above his knee.

"Could this day get any worse," Luke wondered as he struggled to get back on his feet. Taking a first step, his leg felt weak, and he could only limp his way forward. When he finally reached the back of his truck, he had to hang onto the tailgate to stay upright.

It was a short distance to the house. He was so close, yet he felt so far away. All he had to do was get up those steps, onto the porch, and through the door.

On a mental count of three, mustering his last ounce of strength, Luke was off. As he mounted the steps, his leg buckled, and he came crashing down on the wooden porch floor. Using his hands and arms, he desperately clawed his way toward the door.

Melissa heard a loud thud and then Luke yelling in pain. She flung open the door to see he was holding out his hand for help. She reached down and brought him back to his feet. "Luke, what happened?"

"I don't know Mel. I must have caught my foot on a tree root or something. I think I twisted my leg as I fell. It hurts like hell."

"You did more than twist it, Luke. Look at your jeans, you're bleeding. We need to get you inside and out of these wet clothes right away."

As he removed his jeans, they saw a long, deep gash on his leg. "Luke, I need to put some stitches in that cut. I'll go get my emergency kit. Don't move."

Luke felt tired and began to drift off as Melissa hurried out of the room.

"Luke, Luke, wake up." Melissa was sitting with the emergency kit open beside him. She had already threaded a needle and passed it through the flame of a butane lighter. She washed his leg and rubbed alcohol on the area around the cut. Luke hollered out loud with pain as Melissa worked the needle through his skin. "Just two more Luke and then we're done."

"Well Mel," Luke said, grinding his teeth, "they say terrible things come in threes. So, there was this storm, the generator, and me messing up my leg. The good news is that nothing else could possibly go wrong today."

Melissa wrapped a gauze bandage around the wound, holding it in place with adhesive tape. Then she dashed into the kitchen to fetch painkillers and some ice for his swollen leg.

No sooner did Luke say thank you than the telephone rang and pierced the silence in the living room, startling them both. They couldn't think who would be calling them during such a storm, unless it was Luke's parents.

Melissa quickly crossed the room and picked up the phone, "Hello. I'm sorry... whom did you say you were?"

Turning to Luke, her face became pale. Melissa stammered, "There's a Detective Borden on the phone for you. It's about your brother Carson."

"I wonder what that's all about," Luke replied as Melissa handed him the phone.

"Hello, Luke. This is Detective Borden from the Toronto Police Department. Tell me, have you spoken with your brother recently?"

"Not for a while," responded Luke. "Why are you calling and asking about Carson?"

Detective Borden began explaining to Luke what he knew about the shooting in Carson's office, which wasn't very much.

"Hang on a minute, detective. I want to put you on speakerphone. Mel, Carson has been shot at his office in Toronto. Tell me, detective, Doug Anderson is at the same company. Is he okay?"

"Mr. Anderson was on vacation at the time in Hawaii. No one else was hurt. Just your brother. It would appear that he may have been working late, and someone may have broken into the office. We are not sure yet, as we have not had a chance to speak with him, which we hope to do first thing in the morning."

"Can I talk to my brother, detective?"

"That won't be possible right now. Your brother was taken by ambulance to North York General Hospital. The doctors performed emergency surgery and although Carson is out of surgery and in recovery, he is heavily sedated and sleeping at the moment."

"How is Carson's wife, Chelsea holding up?

"We've been trying to reach her for several hours, with no luck so far. We have no idea where she is."

Chapter 12

Juan drove southeast of the heliport at the Toronto Airport to a warehouse and parked the car in an area where it could not be seen from the street. The warehouse had no signage and looked like it was crying out for a much-needed major renovation. The only thing new about this building were the video surveillance cameras anchored to the exterior at strategic locations.

The warehouse was surrounded by mature, overgrown trees, which did little to evoke a feeling of welcome to visitors. The parking lot was broken up with cracks and potholes, half-filled with rainwater.

A rusting metal fence surrounded the property. It was adequate for keeping out the honest but in need of serious repair if it had to keep out anyone intent on getting in.

Locking his car, Juan strolled around the corner of the building, carefully avoiding the water-filled potholes. He thumped on a metal door and waived at the security camera overhead. A minute passed before the door was opened by a burly man. Behind him were two other men armed with M4s.

"Come on in and follow me. Mr. Madler is expecting you."

Stepping inside, Juan could see a dozen men working around large wooden tables. They were busily opening thin metal containers and carefully unloading the contents.

Overhead, on a narrow mezzanine walkway surrounding the interior of the building, he spotted two men surveying the outside perimeter through small upper-level windows. Another two men on the walkway had their eyes glued to the activity happening on the warehouse floor below. Each of them carried M4s at the ready and had radios for communicating with each other and the main office.

A smile came to Juan's face. While the outside of the building looked like it was inhabited by impoverished squatters, the inside was clean, neat, brightly lit, and contained an arsenal of modern weaponry that would be the envy of any country's military. He was going to enjoy his assignment here.

As Juan entered a glass-walled office that overlooked the warehouse floor from the upper mezzanine, Jason Madler rose quickly from his chair behind a large wooden desk to greet him.

"Welcome, Juan. I'm so glad you have arrived safely. Everything is ready for you to begin overseeing the arrival, repackaging, and distribution of your products."

"Thank you. I must say that my first impression of the operation is a good one. You have chosen a perfect facility as our Toronto distribution hub. If the other fa-cilities across the country are set up like this, conditions will be ideal for scaling up our activity."

As Madler escorted Juan on a tour of the warehouse and briefed him on how the operation was proceeding so far, the early afternoon sunlight came through the ceil-ing skylight, splashing all the tables with narrow bands of light, which seemed to dance while the clouds inter-mittently passed by.

Juan carefully observed as bundles of cocaine, heroin, opioids, and fentanyl were being opened by the work-ers at each table and then repackaged into smaller bags. The smaller bags were stuffed carefully into personalized boxes to be transported from the warehouse directly to dealers on the street. The value of drugs on these tables was in the millions and assuming this final test run went smoothly, it would be like this every day from now on. Turning to Madler, he asked, "Is everything in place for distribution from the warehouse to begin?"

"Yes, Juan. Everything is as you requested. Trucks will drive inside the warehouse through these two doors and be loaded with drugs for distribution. Drivers will be given their specific destinations and the route they must follow. They will also be given a password-protected burner phone containing the numbers of contacts they will need to check in with along the route."

"What about the spotters?"

"Spotters will be located at various checkpoints, but the drivers won't know the location of these checkpoints. The spotters will call in the truck's license plate number as it passes each checkpoint. If a truck doesn't pass a checkpoint within specified times, a well-armed search party will be sent to locate it."

Just as Juan was about to respond, a commotion broke out on the main warehouse floor. Two men were yelling loudly, and as they began attacking each other, one table was overturned, spilling an open container of drugs all over the floor.

Rushing in to break up the fight, Juan demanded to know, "Who started this?" Everybody pointed at Harold. Juan turned to Harold, "Is this true? Did you start this fight?"

"Yeah, what of it? And who the hell are you to be questioning what I do?"

Reaching behind his back, without hesitation, Juan pulled out his 9mm Glock and fired two rounds into Harold's forehead. Two red dots instantly appeared, and blood trickled from the holes as Harold fell to the floor with a thud.

There was not another sound to be heard anywhere in the warehouse. Everyone was looking at each other in terror.

Waving his gun so that all could see it, Juan announced, "Mr. Glock and I are the new guys in charge around here. Now clean up this mess and get back to work."

Chapter 13

Borden hung up the phone and sighed as he slumped back into his office desk chair. He had just broken the bad news to his wife that he wouldn't be home for dinner and that their vacation would have to wait.

"That's okay," Lois said after he explained what had happened. "After all these years, I know what it's like being married to a detective. You just be careful and come home when you can."

Borden began to ponder, "Why didn't I just let Cross take the lead on this case? I had already put her in charge. Why does my family always take a back seat to my work? Has my passion for chasing after justice become an obsession?"

His guilt trip was suddenly interrupted by Cross, who came bounding into his office. "Borden, I have good news. Detective Friedman has uncovered some information that could be a breakthrough in the shooting at Complete Real Estate."

A smile came immediately to Borden's face, "Don't keep me in suspense, Cross. What did Friedman find?"

"He canvased the area to find anyone who had video cameras that might have captured a view the street in and around the real estate office. He hit a goldmine at the car dealership directly across the street. One of their cameras provides a head-on view of the exit from the real estate office parking garage. At 3:34 this morning, that camera recorded a Ford Edge SUV leaving the parking garage and heading north. The video is black and white, so we don't have a particular color for the SUV."

"Does the video clearly show the license plate or the driver?"

"Yes, Friedman says you can clearly see the license plate and the faces of two people in the front seat of the vehicle. These could be the ones responsible for the shooting today! And, if so, we now know the approximate time of the shooting. He's headed back to the office now with a copy of the video."

"That's great news, Cross! Get that video to the Tech Team as soon as Friedman gets back. Have them trace the license plate and see if we can get facial recognition on the occupants. With any luck, they may already be in our database."

"One more thing, boss. Detective Kim tracked down the EMS team that picked up Andrea Talbot at the real estate office this morning. At her request, they dropped her off at her home instead of the hospital. They said she was quite adamant about the need to be home."

"Doesn't that seem a bit odd to you, Cross?"

"My thought exactly. And, when Detective Kim went to her house just around the noon hour to interview her about the shooting, he said her reason for coming home was to make sure her daughter was okay. But her daughter was at school, so it doesn't add up."

"Send a unit now to bring Andrea in for questioning."

Chapter 14

Andrea Talbot sat at a table in a tiny room facing a large one-way mirror and the video cameras mounted at the ceiling in two corners. She had not been there long and was drinking a cup of coffee. Borden could see her, but she couldn't see him through the one-way mirror. He watched with interest as the door opened and Cross entered.

"Hi, Andrea. I'm Detective Cross. I saw you at the shooting earlier today. We understand you answered a few questions from Detective Kim, but we just need to tie up some loose ends."

No matter how many times he had seen Cross do this, Borden never tired of watching her in action.

"How are you feeling, Andrea?"

"Okay, I guess."

"Are you married?"

"No, I've been divorced for about seven years now."

Cross opened a file folder and stopped her questioning for about 20 seconds while appearing to read something. Borden could see that Andrea's right eye was starting to twitch. It was a sure sign she was nervous.

"I notice you have a nine-year-old daughter, Andrea, and your ex-husband has visitation rights with her every other week. Is that right?"

"Yes, that's right."

"What's your daughter's name?"

"Her name is Sally."

"That's a beautiful name. What grade is she in?"

"She's in grade 4."

Borden noticed every time Cross asked about Andrea's daughter or talked about her, she began to fidget.

"Andrea, what do you remember from the shooting this morning?"

"Not much. Mr. Blocker and I worked late last night preparing a list of properties for William and Sara Porter to see today. He wanted to make sure everything went smoothly because they were friends of his from back home in Alberta. We agreed to meet again at 8:00 this morning.

"When I got there the door was still locked and the general lighting was still off, so I assumed I was the first to arrive. I made coffee and took some pastries I bought for the meeting down to the boardroom. Then I went to Mr. Blocker's office to get the files we had worked on last night. That's when I found him lying on the floor."

Cross continued, "There were a number of files on the floor in Mr. Blocker's office. Were those the files you prepared for the various properties to view today?"

"I think so."

"What was in those files?"

"Each file contains the usual listing information, like price, property taxes, room measurements, lot size, and pictures of the property. That's all."

"Was there anything particularly outstanding about those properties?"

"Not really. The houses were all well-maintained and offered several amenities."

"Is there any financial information about the clients in these files?"

Andrea paused before answering, "That information is confidential and normally kept at the office, in our main database. Sometimes information is printed, but it is typically kept in a locked and secured filing cabinet."

"Who has the key to that filing cabinet, Andrea?"

"I have a key. So does Mr. Blocker and Doug Anderson."

"So," Cross continued, "if you wanted to search your database you could link up a property worth, say four million dollars, and all clients in your database who could afford to purchase a property like that, is that correct?"

"Yes, that's correct."

"Are you all right, Andrea? You seem nervous or up-set. Are you worried about something? When does your daughter get back from school today?"

"She'll be home within an hour."

There it is, Borden realized. He could see a tear form-ing in her eye. Something is going on, and it concerns her daughter.

"Andrea, do you want a tissue?" Cross asked. "Is something bothering you? You can trust me. I can help you if there is a problem."

"How long do I need to stay here, detective? I want to go home."

"Can I get you another cup of coffee, Andrea? I need one myself too. I'll be right back."

Chapter 15

Joining Borden in the room behind the one-way mirror, Cross exclaimed, "There's something about her daughter that has her worried, Borden."

"I saw that too. But I don't think that's all she's worried about. While you were questioning Andrea, I received a report from the Forensic Team regarding their investigation of the computers at Complete Real Estate. Andrea made a copy of the entire office database."

"Are you serious? Did she copy all the client's personal information?"

"Yes, she did."

"Why would she do that, Borden? Was she forced to make a copy?"

"Let's assume for the time being that she was forced to make a copy. You need to get back in there and find out why, and to whom she was going to give the information."

A few minutes later, Detective Cross re-entered the room, carrying two fresh coffees.

"Andrea, I have just a few more questions for you and then we can wrap this up."

"I hope so detective, I need to get back to my daughter. She will be home from school soon."

"Tell me, Andrea, why did you make a copy of the financial records of all the clients in the company database?"

Andrea looked stunned. Breaking down into tears, she stammered, "How do you know about that?"

"Tell me what happened," pleaded Cross.

"I can't tell you!"

"Why can't you tell me?"

"I can't tell you because they will hurt my daughter. They threatened to kill her."

"Who threatened you? Who will hurt your daughter, Andrea? Tell me his name."

"I don't know his name. A man called me several days ago at the office and said if I didn't do exactly what he told me to do, he would hurt my daughter. He said he knew where I lived and what school my daughter attends, and one day she wouldn't come home if I didn't do what he said. He told me to make a copy of the entire office database and put it on a flash drive.

"At first, I told him I couldn't do that. I didn't have access to the database. I didn't have a password to do that and could only access a limited number of things on any given day.

"He told me that wasn't a problem. I would receive a flash drive that evening at my house, and all I had to do was slip it into the USB port of my office computer. He said it would take care of everything.

"I didn't want to do it. I knew it was wrong, but he left me no choice. He said Sally's life depended on me doing exactly as he said. He even knew the name of her teacher at school, and where she went to play with her friends." Andrea began sobbing uncontrollably.

Borden grabbed his phone and called for a police-woman to immediately locate Sally Talbot at her school and bring her safely back to the station.

Cross knew precisely what Borden was doing at that very moment because she would have done the same thing. Don't worry about your daughter, Andrea. We are bringing her back to the station now and she will be with you within the hour."

"Thank you, detective. I just have to protect my daughter. The man who called me said if I told any-one at the office, the police, or anyone else, whatever happened to my daughter would be my fault. If I said anything, he would know about it."

Breaking down into tears, once again, it was obvious Andrea would not be able to continue much longer.

"Just a few more questions. Then you'll be able to see your daughter. You said the man sent you a flash drive to use when you downloaded the information from the database. How was the person you spoke to going to get the flash drive from you?"

"Well, the man called me just before Mr. Blocker and I began reviewing properties for the Porters late yesterday afternoon. He told me to put the flash drive into a plain white envelope and wait for further instructions."

"What happened next, Andrea?"

"I told him I wouldn't give him the files. He started yelling at me and started swearing so I hung up the phone. My daughter was staying with my ex-husband last night, so I knew she would still be safe until I could see her again and figure out what to do next."

"So, the man didn't get the flash drive. Where is it now, Andrea?"

"I still have it." Reaching for her purse, Andrea took out the flash drive and handed it to Detective Cross.

"Has anyone seen what is on this drive, Andrea?"

"No, nobody has seen the drive or even knows that I have it except you and that evil man. Am I in trouble, detective?"

"We need to wait until the investigation is over before I can answer that, but in the meantime, we are putting you and your daughter in a safe house with round-the-clock protection.

"Right now, I need you to hand me your cell phone so our Forensic Team can check it for clues about who called you. We'll give it back to you before you leave.

"I need you to listen very carefully to what I say next, Andrea. You must not use your cell phone to send or receive calls until this case is solved. The man who called you might be able to track your location if you do. If the man contacts you on your cell phone again, I want you to answer the call and keep him talking for as long as you can, so we can trace it. I want you to agree to do whatever he asks.

"Before you leave here today, we'll also be giving you a burner phone. Detective Borden and I will be the only people from this office to speak with you on that phone. Do not give out the phone number to anyone. Not to your ex-husband, your parents, or anyone at your office. If you give this number to anyone, you could be putting yourself and your daughter in danger."

Chapter 16

Borden and Cross drove up the driveway of the Carson house and parked behind a police cruiser. "How ironic is this, Cross? We've been searching everywhere for Chelsea Blocker, and it was her that reached out to us."

Even before they could ring the doorbell, a female constable was opening the door. "Detective Borden, Mrs. Blocker is expecting you. I told her you were the lead detective investigating the shooting of her husband. She's in the family room, just at the end of the hall and through the door on your right."

Entering the family room, Borden and Cross saw a distraught, impeccably dressed woman sitting alone, staring blankly out a window that overlooked a well-manicured lawn, an in-ground swimming pool, and a large patio area.

"Good day, Mrs. Blocker."

Hearing a voice, Chelsea Blocker got up from her chair and turned to see who it was.

"I'm Detective Borden and this is my partner, Detective Cross. I understand you recently had a break-in."

Before Borden could say another word, Chelsea walked past them and headed for the door they had just entered. She stopped and turned around. "Follow me!"

She led them down a different hallway to the rear of the house and into a large square kitchen, which one would expect to see in a fancy restaurant.

Without speaking, she pointed to a broken window-pane in a large French door, which led from the kitchen to a covered back porch.

"Mrs. Blocker—" said Borden. That was as far as he got.

"Please call me Chelsea," She extended a hand to both detectives.

Borden continued, "Chelsea, are you okay?"

"No, detective. I am very anxious right now.

"I'm worried sick about my husband.

"Is he okay?

"I don't feel safe in this house anymore.

"Do you know if I can go to see my husband?

"Is he going to be all right?

"Do you think I should stay here?

"Do you think the person who broke in here will come back?"

"Those are all good questions, Chelsea. We will answer them shortly, but we need to ask you a few questions about the break-in first. Tell me, do you know what time the break-in occurred?"

"I was out of town yesterday visiting a friend in Chicago. I flew home late last night and went directly to bed. Early this morning, I went to breakfast with a friend.

"Then I did some clothes shopping before heading off to meet another friend for a late lunch. When I returned home just after 3:30, I came into the kitchen to make a cup of tea. That's when I discovered my French door window was broken, and the door unlocked. So quite frankly, I don't know when the break-in occurred.

"I called 911, and the police car outside showed up minutes later. The female constable told me right away that my husband had been shot and that the police were trying to contact me. I forgot to charge my cell phone when I got home last night, and the battery went dead, so that's why you couldn't reach me. I feel so terrible about all this. Detective Borden, please tell me what's going on."

"Chelsea, here is what we know so far. Your husband was shot while in his office early this morning or during the night. He was taken to North York General Hospital and fortunately for him, the injury was not life-threatening. He is expected to make a complete recovery."

"Oh, my goodness. Who would do such a terrible thing?"

"That's what we would like to know, Chelsea," Cross said. "Do you know of anyone who would want to hurt your husband?"

"No, no, everyone liked Carson. I can't believe someone would want to hurt him, let alone shoot him. Why would someone shoot my husband? Why?"

Cross answered, "We don't know, but we are going to find the answer to that question. Perhaps you could answer a few more questions for us? I know this is personal, but it's all part of our investigation. We understand you and your husband are getting a divorce."

"No, detective, we have temporarily separated, but I expect we'll work through our differences. It's just that he spends so much time at work that he has little time for anything else. For now, I live here in the house, and Carson lives in the guest house over the garage."

Cross continued, "Do you know if anyone threatened your husband lately or if he has any enemies? Did your husband ever mention that he was having problems with anyone at work or elsewhere?"

"No, on both counts," Chelsea replied.

Borden interjected, "Chelsea, I want to ask you a few questions to figure out if robbery was a motive in this break-in. Do you or your husband keep a large amount of cash in the house, or do you have a lot of jewelry or anything else of value here?"

"We don't keep a lot of cash in the house, but both my husband and I have separate safes where we keep our own money, jewelry, or whatever else we might want to protect."

"Can you tell me if anything is missing?" asked Borden.

"I don't know. I haven't spent much time looking around the house. I just got back from Chicago as I mentioned. I know the safes are intact, but I can't tell if anything is missing just yet."

"Do you or your husband have any computers?"

"Yes, we both have laptop computers here in the house. We normally keep them in our home offices. Both Carson and I have separate offices. He uses the office here because there is a problem with the Internet in the guest house."

"Are the computers missing or are they still here?"

"I'm not sure, detective. I haven't used mine for several days and I guess it's still in my office."

"Could you take me to the home offices, Chelsea? I would like to know if the computers are here."

"Follow me, detectives."

Cross followed Borden and Chelsea out of the kitchen and down another hallway. Although the two home offices were in the same part of the house, they were separated by a sliding glass wall.

They walked into one of the offices, which Chelsea said belonged to Carson. "That's strange," she said, "Carson's laptop isn't here."

"Chelsea could Carson have taken his laptop to work?" asked Borden.

"That wouldn't make any sense, because he has another laptop computer that he mainly uses at work."

Opening the sliding glass wall and stepping into her office, Chelsea exclaimed, "I can't believe it. My laptop is gone too!"

She sat on a couch, and Borden and Cross sat directly opposite her on two leather chairs.

Cross knew it was her turn to ask some personal questions that always upset people. "Chelsea, we need look at all the angles concerning Carson's shooting. Does your husband have any gambling debts?"

"No, of course not. Why do you even ask such a question?"

"It's routine. Just trying to eliminate possible motives for everything that happened today. Does anyone have a grudge against your husband?"

"I think you already asked me that question. Why would anyone have a grudge against Carson? Everyone liked him and he got along with everyone."

Cross was thankful she was getting to the end of her questions. "How long have you been married? Again, this is just a routine question."

"Why would you want to know how long we've been married? We have been married for over three years and we recently separated, as I already mentioned to you earlier."

Borden could see Chelsea was getting agitated and knew it was time to back off. "That's all the questions we have for now." He took a card from his pocket and handed it to Chelsea. "If you think of anything else that might be helpful, please contact us."

Chapter 17

After a restless night's sleep pondering the details of the case so far, Borden decided to head into the office early. He couldn't help thinking that today he was supposed to be heading up to his cottage to spend the next four weeks on a stress-free vacation.

His first stop was to the Tech Team to get an update on the video that Detective Friedman had uncovered.

"We've got good news for you, Borden. Everything came together about half an hour ago. We enhanced the video from the car dealership and using our face recognition software, we were able to identify the two individuals in the SUV. We also ran the plates on the vehicle, and we have an address for the registered owner. Here's our full report."

Eagerly accepting the file, Borden headed straight to his office to study all the details and figure out his next move. It was 8:00 a.m. on the dot when he saw Cross coming toward his office.

"Great news, Cross. The video gave us everything we needed to track down that SUV and, hopefully, the shooting suspects. According to our intel, these guys are repeat offenders, and although the SUV wasn't registered in their name, we have the address of where they've been living for at least a year.

"The first suspect is Stan Temple, 36, who is well-known to several police forces in the US and Canada. Stan has a lengthy list of offenses and was suspected of being an enforcer for the Perrett family in New York. He'd shoot his mother for $50 if he needed the cash.

"The second suspect is his brother, Derek Temple, 33, also well-known to police on both sides of the border. Derek has been arrested on a host of different charges, dating back to when he was a teenager. He is also known to be well-versed in computer technology, a skill he picked up during his last stint in prison. He idolizes his big brother Stan.

"I've spent the last two hours organizing a team to pay our suspects an early-morning surprise visit. They'll be you and me, Detectives Kim and Friedman, and four uniformed police constables, including Gibson and Grant, participating in this operation. The team is mobilizing now to assemble at a parking lot close to the location. Grab your gear, and let's go."

During the drive to the assembly area, Borden and Cross discussed the case. "Borden, why would these two men be breaking into the offices of Complete Real Estate? I don't see anything in the intel on their backgrounds that has anything to do with real estate?"

"Good question, Cross. And why did they target Complete Real Estate? Why not other offices? Why did

Carson Blocker get shot? Did he know these men, or was he just in the wrong place at the wrong time?"

Arriving at the assembly area in the parking lot of a vacant retail outlet four blocks from the suspects' location, Borden's team exited their vehicles for a last-minute briefing.

Pointing to Constables Gibson and Grant, Borden spoke in a voice of authority, "You two will enter from the back of the house. Detectives Kim and Friedman will enter from the front, while Cross and I enter to cover the side entrance."

Pointing to the two remaining uniformed constables, he continued, "You two will act as backup using scoped rifles in case we need cover fire. Everyone trust your instincts on this one and be prepared for anything. These two are considered armed and dangerous. Move out and take up your positions."

Chapter 18

It had been raining earlier in the morning, and dark clouds still cast a gloomy light on the house of Stan and Derek Temple as the tactical team moved quietly on foot toward the house from all sides, with weapons ready.

The south-facing house looked normal. It was a two-story wooden structure on an expansive lot with a few mature trees and a poorly kept garden of perennial flowers.

The sound of singing robins could be heard in the trees, but otherwise, the surrounding neighborhood remained quiet. The only sign that Stan and Derek were there was a black Ford Edge SUV parked at the front of the house. Using binoculars, Borden confirmed it was the vehicle suspected of being involved in yesterday's shooting.

Borden felt the adrenaline begin to pulsate through his body. He spoke softly into his communication device, "Unlock weapons. We go on my command."

Just then, he heard a buzzing sound overhead. He looked up to see a drone flying in large circles just east of the house. "Why would there be a drone in the area?" he wondered.

An instant later, without warning, the cloudy morning sky lit up as three massive floodlights strobed on and off, momentarily blinding everyone.

Then came a clatter of rapid gunfire from within the house, shattering the windows into hundreds of tiny lethal projectiles. Bullets began ricocheting off the Temple brother's black SUV, exploding all the windows.

Borden and his team instinctively dove to the ground and scrambled to shelter behind the trees. They returned gunfire to first knock out the floodlights, then continued shooting in the direction of the house to an unseen target.

The sound of more windows shattering and wood breaking off the lap-straight siding seemed never-ending.

Then a projectile came blazing out the front window of the house and hit the gas tank of the SUV, blowing it up and into the sky. It rolled over in mid-air and exploded into a massive fireball, with its bulky frame and dozens of smaller parts falling to the ground in flames.

Fireworks began exploding in all directions from inside the house in a continuous stream, once again pinning the task force to the ground. It was a massive show of confusion and terror at the same time.

As the fireworks subsided, Borden looked up to see flames engulfing the inside of the house. Thick black smoke began billowing out the now glassless windows, soon making it impossible to see the building or its surroundings clearly.

In the distance, the sound of firetrucks with their distinct sirens could be heard blaring and growing louder as they hurried toward the war zone.

Cautiously, Borden got up off the ground and looked in the direction of Cross, "What the hell just happened?" Looking around, he counted each member of the task force as they slowly rose to their feet. He breathed a noticeable sigh of relief when he realized everyone was still alive. A few of them had cuts and bruises, but nothing serious.

The house had burned hot, and it was obvious that nobody would be exiting that building alive. When the fire crew arrived, they were quick to pour water on the area around the house and into what remained of the home to ensure the fire didn't spread.

Borden spoke into his headset, "Okay, everyone, meet me back behind the cars." As they gathered where Borden stood, he began barking out orders.

"All uniformed constables secure the area to make sure no unauthorized people get in or out of here. All detectives fan out and begin investigating the area surrounding the property to see if there are any clues about what's going on here."

Slowly but surely, neighbors started trickling out of their houses and heading to see what all the commotion was about. "What a shame," the neighbors said to one another. "The whole house went up in smoke, and look what happened to their SUV. The two brothers who lived here were such nice boys. Do you think they were inside? Are they still alive?"

Borden pulled a bullhorn from his car and yelled into it louder than needed, mainly because he wasn't hearing that well after all the explosions.

"This is a crime scene and a restricted area. Everyone please go back to your homes and stay inside. We'll instruct you when it's safe to leave your house."

From the opposite side of the property, Detective Friedman hollered out, "Borden, come here. You have to see this."

As Borden approached, he could see Cross walking into what appeared to be a hole in the ground. When he got to where Friedman was standing, there was a moment of astonishment as he realized it was more than just a hole. It was an escape tunnel from the house.

Friedman pointed out fresh tire marks exiting the tunnel. "It looks like these were made by two lightweight motorcycles."

Borden nodded in agreement. "This whole thing was a cleverly crafted diversion to cover their escape."

Chapter 19

Borden ended the call with a quick click on his cell phone. "That was the hospital, Cross. The doctor said that because Carson was unconscious for about five hours, he sustained a moderate brain injury from the blow to his head. He wants Carson to rest in relative silence for two more days to allow his brain to recover from post-traumatic amnesia and return to logical thought processes."

"That won't be a problem," said Cross. "Our priority right now is finding the Temple brothers."

Borden twisted his head to glance over his shoulder at the smoldering house. It had been hosed down many times during the past hour. Police were meticulously combing the ruins while firefighters continued to douse small pockets of flames. Steam continued to rise from the ashes wherever water hit the few remaining hot spots.

"Cross, have Kim and Friedman check with any residences or businesses in the area to see if they have video footage of two motorcycles leaving this vicinity around the time of the calamity here. Also, check with the Department of Highways and see if there are any highway cams in the area which show one or two motorcycles going in any direction. The Temple brothers may have split up, so have them flag any motorcycle in this area up to the present time."

While he had been issuing his orders to Cross, Borden noticed someone poking around the remains of the house interior. He felt instant relief when he realized it was Terry O'Connor. If anyone could unravel what happened here, it would be him. Not only was he the Fire Chief, but Borden knew that Terry was considered one of the best arson specialists in all of Canada.

Terry moved swiftly toward Borden with a hand extended. "Detective Borden, good to see that you and your team appear to be fine." The Chief was not known as a chit-chat type of person, but one who always cut quickly to the point.

"My initial assessment is that the house was deliberately torched and in addition, I concluded that the arrival of the police was expected. There were, until the fire, of course, multiple boxes of fireworks upstairs and on the main floor. If we can trace the origin of the fireworks or where they were purchased, I'll let you know."

Borden looked to see if Cross was still standing there and was glad she was. She was writing furiously as the Chief continued his monologue.

"We were able to determine they used a highly flammable accelerant, likely paint thinner, which they poured throughout the upper area of the house as well as the main floor, but not in the basement. This stuff is readily available at any hardware store or big-box retailer.

"The fire started in the kitchen using a toaster, which had a timer attached to it. The toaster was at the edge of the counter, and all indications are that they weren't toasting bread, but probably some paper towel. When the paper towel caught fire, it fell off the counter to the floor. From there, the accelerant spread the fire throughout the main floor and up the staircase to the second floor. It was a clever plan to use fireworks and guns as a stalling ploy.

"Oh, and one more interesting thing, there's an opening in the basement wall hidden by a bookcase, which leads to a tunnel that travels out and away from the house. It then exits behind the garage near the far edge of the property. The way it was constructed and camouflaged, it was so well hidden that I don't think anyone would have ever stumbled upon it, even if they were looking for a tunnel. I assume that's how your fugitives made their escape."

Borden thanked the Chief for the information and motioned to Cross to join him as he headed toward the charcoal skeleton of a house.

Turning back toward the Chief, Borden asked, "Is it okay to enter what's left of the building?"

"Sure, but be careful. The structure is weak and could collapse. It would be best if you waited until tomorrow when everything has cooled down completely. But I know you have a job to do."

Carefully walking into what had been the living room, Borden and Cross noticed the remains of a large screen television, and some springs and wireframe which had once been a couch.

Then Borden saw a blackened rifle mounted on a tripod connected to what looked like a motor. "Cross, thankfully, those guys bought high-quality equipment made of metal instead of plastic, which would have melted in all the heat. As for the motor, if that's what it was, it could have allowed someone to operate the gun from a remote location."

Borden then looked up toward the second floor and noticed something unusual. Grabbing a ladder that the Chief had left behind, Borden leaned it against the floorboards of the second floor and climbed up gingerly, one step at a time.

"Hey, Cross you need to look at this. This is un-believable."

Just then, the floorboard supporting the ladder snapped. Borden's attempt to grab hold of a vertical post failed as he fell backward off the ladder and crashed to the floor with a thud, hitting his head on a charred 2X4.

Cross yelled to one of the firefighters on the other side of the room, who dashed to his truck to grab an emergency first aid kit. Borden was startled by the fall, and the firefighter put a bandage on the back of his head to stop the bleeding.

Cross leaned over Borden and asked, "Are you okay? I think I should call for an ambulance."

"No Cross. Don't call EMS! They'll want to take me to the hospital to make sure I'm okay. The wait time to see a doctor could be hours wasted and this investigation could go cold. The sooner we wrap this case up, the better. I'll have plenty of time to rest up on my vacation, assuming I ever get there. I'm probably going to have a headache. No big deal. Now if you could please help me up, we can get back to work."

Thanking the firefighter for his help, Borden once again turned his attention to Cross. "What I saw, before I fell, was the remains of a rifle with a large clip mounted on a tripod. It was probably an M4. This gun was pointed at the location of the SUV and had what looked like a small motor that might have been connected by Wi-Fi to give someone the ability to control it remotely. I'm not sure, we'll have to wait and see what the Forensic Team comes back with."

Walking through the rubble, Borden and Cross made their way into the basement to examine the entrance to the tunnel behind the bookcase that Terry had mentioned. Entering the tunnel and following it all the way to the exit at the far edge of the property, they were surprised at how well it was constructed.

"Cross does this situation remind you of anything?"

"It certainly looks like a page from the Mexican Cartel playbook to me. They have a thing for using tunnels to escape being captured when police raid their hideaways."

"Exactly what I was thinking, Cross. If the Temple brothers are working for the Cartel, this case is bigger than we thought."

Chapter 20

After exiting their escape tunnel under cover of the pandemonium Derek had triggered from his cell phone just moments before, the Temple brothers casually rode their quiet electric motorcycles at the speed limit through the neighboring streets behind their house. The last thing they wanted was to attract attention to themselves and where they were going.

Following a carefully pre-planned route to avoid traffic cameras, they navigated their way to the country roads just north of the city, where their movement would be almost impossible to trace. Turning into a dirt laneway leading to an abandoned farmhouse, they spotted a cube van with its back overhead door open waiting to welcome them.

Stan and Derek each slowly guided their motorcycles straight up the lowered ramp into the cargo box and turned off their motors. Jumping to the ground, they closed and locked the back door of the van.

The driver and his companion lowered their windows as they watched both men in the side-view mirrors walking up either side of the van.

Speaking to Stan, the driver asked, "How did things go back at the safe house?"

"It was like the Fourth of July on steroids. Just like we planned it. Thanks to both of you for your help yesterday setting up Madler's care package you brought from the warehouse."

Derek chirped, "Yeah, the drone worked like a charm. We had a front-row seat watching the cops approach on the big screen TV in the living room."

"Madler will be happy to hear this," said the man in the passenger seat. "Here are the keys to the car I drove here for you. There's a new burner phone on the front seat. Madler wants you to call him right away. You'll find a small arsenal and a new drone in the trunk to replace what you lost in your escape."

"Thanks," said Stan. "You guys leave first, and we'll head out after I speak to Madler."

Climbing into the front seat of the car, Stan immediately picked up the phone and punched the number for Madler's burner. "Hey boss, the escape went as planned. I was told to call you right away."

"While the two of you are in the country north of the city, I need you to head over to the property owned by Bob Jackson. The directions will be in the envelope I left along with your new burner phone. It's not that far from where you are. I want you to scout out the location to make sure when he is home, where you can spot him, and where you won't be seen in case we need to take action to protect our interests."

"Yes sir, I understand," replied Stan just before disconnecting the call. Starting the car, he said, "We have a new assignment, Derek. We have to go to a property nearby owned by this guy named Jackson. The address is in the envelope Madler left for us. Punch it into the GPS and let's get this over with so we can go grab something to eat."

Reaching their destination, the brothers casually drove by the entrance to the property. Experience had taught them to approach and leave a location without being detected or drawing suspicion.

"Stan, the boys from the warehouse left a drone in the back of the car. Why don't you pull over and I'll fly the drone so that we can look at all the roads surrounding the house and scout a location for whatever we have to do if we come back? It will only take a couple of minutes. A property that large may have people working in and around it, so we better make sure that there is nobody there before we check it out."

"Good idea Derek. I'll pull over a short way up the road and you can take care of it. We can examine the footage later."

After several minutes of video recording the area using the drone, Stan drove back to the Jackson house, up the driveway, and parked at the front of his house. They wanted their tour of the place to appear as if two friends were dropping by for a visit. Derek knocked on the door. If anyone answered, they would say they were looking for a Tom Hamilton and ask if he lived here. Of course, the answer would be no, they would leave, and nobody would be the least bit skeptical.

Since no one answered the door, they quickly walked around the house, looking through all the windows. Using his cell phone, Stan took pictures of the inside and outside of the house as best he could. He hoped the photos might help him draw a layout of all the rooms with windows.

From what they observed through the windows, they knew the house was clean and tidy, with no signs of toys or items belonging to small children. That was good news. Children would complicate their plans.

In one room at the side of the house, with an expansive window, there was a computer screen on a modern glass desk. Stan figured this was the home office that Jackson used.

Outside that window, at the back of the house, was an outdoor entertainment area featuring a large barbecue, several comfortable-looking lounge chairs, and an inground swimming pool. Under a covered deck area was a large flat-screen television mounted to a wall. Below the television was a built-in pizza oven behind a very smart-looking bar area. This house screamed money, lots of money. Stan figured it must be worth a fortune.

Having taken all the pictures and drone footage they needed while ensuring they didn't get any dirt on their shoes or leave any footprints in the gardens or on the walkways, the pair returned to their car, turned it around in the driveway, and headed back to the country road.

Turning right, they drove a short distance before spotting an opening among the trees and underbrush with an old grass-covered driveway. The driveway seemed to be an entrance to a farmer's field, used years ago, perhaps even before Bob Jackson bought his property.

By the amount of underbrush and grass on the pathway, it didn't seem like this entrance had experienced any recent use. Stan figured it would be a perfect area to set up if Madler wanted him to take action. He parked at the side of the road, and after taking a quick walk to check the view to Jackson's house, Stan knew they had what they came for.

Chapter 21

Madler entered the warehouse, nodding to the armed guard who was standing by to close and bolt the door behind him. As he strolled casually toward his office, he watched four of his men working diligently around a large table.

Fake driver's licenses, health cards, passports, and credit cards were being made to order and packaged for delivery to clients all over the world using personal information gleaned from stolen computers and USB drives.

Madler could not suppress his grin of self-satisfaction. Identity theft and fraud were his babies. This is the operation that made him a small fortune before being recruited by Carlos Martinez and his connections at the Mexican Cartel to organize the packaging and distribution of their drugs in Canada.

Entering his glass-walled office on the mezzanine, he found his right-hand man, Vincent, waiting patiently for him to arrive.

"Do you have the file on the Peterson property, Vincent?"

"Yes sir, everything is set for whatever action you want to take."

"Call our contact at the bank and start proceedings to borrow money for a major house renovation, including a new barn with horse stalls to accommodate eight racehorses.

"Transfer the property into the name of Kenneth Dunbar. Tell our contact to put a rush on the paperwork because we need an immediate advance of $2.0 million into our account today.

"If our contact asks, tell him it's an advance we need to pay for architect fees, engineering plans, environmental studies, building permits, construction deposits, cost of materials to be shipped, and other incidentals. All of it is required by law. We have to follow the law, right?

"Remind him to use the existing appraisal of $18 million to substantiate the loan. Tell him that the total amount we need only requires an increase of $6.0 million to the existing mortgage. The appraisal on the property is in the file and the bank has a copy since they did the original appraisal."

Madler continued. "In this package, we have fake background information, including credit cards made out to Kenneth Dunbar, along with his passport, Nexus card, social insurance number, and tax returns for the last four years showing he earns more than $9.5 million a year.

"This is priority number one, Vincent. You need to get on with this immediately!"

Vincent replied, "This is routine stuff. There should be no problem."

"I have a smaller project I'd also like you to tackle," said Madler. There's a house in Leaside we need to place a mortgage on. Here's the folder, and you'll note that a certified appraisal by the bank values the property at $5.4 million.

"I want you to transfer the title of the property to Daniel Wise, a self-made millionaire investment broker. All the fake background information you'll need is included in this file. Because there's no existing mortgage on the property, this should be straightforward. Ask for a mortgage of $1.2 million on the property to cover the cost of an outdoor pool and entertainment area, as well as an extension to the back of the house. A further interior renovation will include a new kitchen, finishing the basement, installation of metal shingles, and all new windows throughout the house.

"Request our contact to transfer $500 thousand immediately into our account. Tell him the architect, interior designer, and contractors all need money upfront before they can start the project."

Nodding his head in agreement, Vincent replied, "Consider it done. By the way, my follow-up discussion with Bob Jackson did not go as planned. He's getting cold feet and doesn't want to approve any more mortgage deals."

"Thanks for the update, Vincent. It's too bad that Bob wants out. He's made a small fortune from his cut of all the deals he's slipped through for us so far. I'm really going to miss him."

Chapter 22

Answering his burner phone, Stan listened intently as Madler said in a matter-of-fact tone, "Jackson has become a loose end. You need to take action right away."

Leaving their safehouse in The Beaches area of Toronto, it took almost an hour for Stan and Derek to reach the country estate of Bob Jackson. Passing the driveway, they could see a gleaming BMW parked in front of the garage doors.

"This is good," said Stan. "Jackson's somewhere in the house."

When they reached the well-hidden grass-covered driveway they had discovered the day before, Derek turned off the engine. He and his brother sat in silence for a few minutes.

"Stan," Derek said quietly. "Have you ever felt wrong about the things you've done in the past? I mean, you've killed people. Did it ever make you feel bad? Is it the same as when you intentionally hurt someone, or are those feelings different?"

"Shut up, Derek. I don't want to talk about it or even think about it. What do you think? You have blood on your hands as well. Now shut up. It's time to do the job we're paid to do, which is to please Madler."

"Who cares if we please Madler? Maybe we're in over our heads, Stan. Have you ever thought of quitting and doing something different? To go somewhere nobody knows you?"

"Of course, I've considered that, but I don't let my thoughts run away from the job at hand."

"Stan, what's preventing us from turning this car around right now and leaving? Who cares about Madler? At some point, this is all going to end with us in prison or dead. I don't like it. I don't enjoy hurting people or killing anyone. Maybe it's time for us to think about ourselves and what we're going to do with the rest of our lives. Why are we always taking orders from Madler?"

"Because Madler's the boss, and he pays us well. That's why we take orders from him. Now shut up, Derek."

But Derek would not give up that easily. "You're right, Madler has paid us well. We have more than enough money saved already to make a fresh start in another country. Why don't we go live in Australia or South America?"

"You're talking crazy, Derek. You make it sound like we're millionaires. We don't have nearly enough money to just up and walk away yet."

"Then let's give ourselves one more big payday. You know the schedule of the trucks that are carrying drugs, and where those trucks are headed across Canada, don't you? We could easily hijack a truck, take the drugs and sell them on the street, and make enough money to disappear into the night."

"No, Derek. Madler has never told me anything about the drug side of the operation. When I asked him about it, he told me it was on a need-to-know basis, and I didn't need to know.

"And besides, Madler is in bed with the Cartel now. If we ever stole anything from them, they'd put out contracts to hunt us down and kill us on sight. Don't forget what they've done in the past. They kill traitors in front of their families, and then they kill their entire family."

Stan was starting to worry that his brother was losing his mind. "The last thing either of us needs right now, Derek, is to get in the bad books of the Cartel. You must never mention a word of this conversation to anyone, or I may have to kill you myself. No one must ever know about this conversation. Is that clear? If anyone finds out about it, we will both be killed."

Chapter 23

While Stan cleared a spot in the woods to set things up, Derek prepared for a speedy getaway by turning the car around and backing it slowly down the grass-covered driveway. He muttered under his breath as he broke a few low-hanging branches off the trees that would keep the car hidden from the roadway.

Turning off the engine, he lit a cigarette and took a long deep drag. Stan hated it when he smoked, but Derek found it relaxing, and after the conversation they had just finished, he needed a little time to calm down and collect his thoughts.

A minute later, Derek popped the trunk and took out an orange beach towel and a black duffle bag. Quietly closing the trunk, he took one last drag of his cigarette. Instinctively, he threw the butt onto the ground and stepped on it while twisting his foot before walking deeper into the woods to join Stan.

"Okay, Derek, this is the spot." Stan was looking at the ranch house, contemplating what he had to do.

Derek spread the oversized beach towel neatly on some leaves and twigs and placed the large duffel bag beside it.

Unzipping the duffle bag, Stan began assembling the rifle parts it was carrying as he had done so many times before. After clipping the scope into place and screwing on the silencer, he fastened a short tripod to the barrel.

Laying down on the large towel, Stan opened the tripod legs and adjusted their position to give him a level view. The air was still, so the wind would not be a factor. He calculated the bullet would drop two degrees over the distance from where he was, across the field and the backyard patio that was directly in line with Jackson's home office window.

Stan looked through his scope and adjusted it to raise the crosshairs a fraction.

"Jackson just walked past the window. He's in his office. Get ready to make the phone call Derek. As soon as I get up after taking the shot, pick up the shell casing and the beach towel and head back to the car. I'll dismantle the gun and put it back in the duffle bag. Have the engine running and be ready to go as soon as I drop the bag in the trunk. When you take off, be sure to drive at the speed limit and don't draw any attention to us."

Looking back through the scope, Stan remembered the configuration of Jackson's office from the photo he had taken yesterday. "If Jackson is sitting at his desk, Derek I'll never have a clear shot. I need him to look out the window."

Tapping the number he already had set on his burner phone, Derek called Bob Jackson's cell. "Hello, Mr. Jackson. I'm outside your house right now. I have a delivery for you and was asked to leave it on your back patio. Where exactly would you like me to put it?"

Seconds later, Bob Jackson was peering out his office window, and his head was square in Stan's crosshairs.

Chapter 24

After a restless night of tossing and turning in bed, pondering the details of the case, Borden rose early and headed into the office to meet with the team and compare notes. In the middle of the debriefing session, his administrative assistant, Caroline, knocked on the conference room door.

"I'm sorry to interrupt, Detective Borden, but three federal agents are waiting for you in your office. I told them you were in an important meeting, but they insisted that they had to see you now."

Adjourning the meeting, Borden wondered what else could possibly happen to delay his vacation. As he walked back into his office, he stopped to glare at his uninvited guests. "Happy Sunday," he said with all the sarcasm he could muster. "What's so important that you hauled me out of a meeting?"

Borden was about to sit down when one of the two men stood, stuck out his hand, and introduced himself. "I'm Sergeant Rick Crawford with the RCMP. This is my partner Sergeant Charles Westwood, and this is Agent Danielle Spade from CSIS."

"CSIS? You just got my attention. What's going on in my jurisdiction that's of interest to the Canadian Security Intelligence Service?"

"We understand you've had a very busy two days, detective," said Sergeant Crawford.

"What makes you think that?" answered Borden.

Crawford continued, "We have learned of the break-in and theft of computers from the real estate office in North York. We have had similar incidents involving real estate firms in Edmonton and Calgary during the past six months."

Westwood interjected, "We also believe this is the same group that has been active in both Vancouver and Victoria. And we've been working closely with Agent Spade, who has a team investigating and tracking a terrorist group from Mexico that has moved into Canada during the past year."

"We believe that this terrorist group is somehow connected to the real estate break-ins, and a complex web of identity theft and fraud." added Spade. "We suspect they are using the money from their fraudulent activities to finance their terrorist operation."

"What kind of fraudulent activities?" asked Borden.

"Here's where it gets interesting," said Crawford. It's not just the counterfeit credit cards and passports we usually encounter with identity theft. Multi-million-dollar properties are being refinanced using fake documents. After negotiating a higher mortgage on these properties using these documents, they receive the money from the bank or trust company.

"With the cash in hand, they walk away from the assets leaving the various financial institutions and owners with the debt.

"The reason they give the banks for increasing the mortgage usually involves extensive home renovations. We suspect they have accomplices in the banking industry, but we haven't been able to prove anything yet."

Borden reflected for a moment on what he had just heard. "So how does all this fit in with the real estate office break-ins you mentioned?"

Westwood was the next to speak. "Every real estate transaction requires the buyers and sellers to provide every piece of personal information that anyone would ever need to create a fake identity. So, breaking into real estate offices to steal their computers is a gold mine for fraudsters."

Before anybody else could speak, Borden held up his hands. "I don't doubt what you are saying. You have done plenty of work on this. I thought we were simply dealing with some local and highly organized gang at Friday's break-in and shooting. Now you're telling me this is part of a massive operation that's active, not just across Canada, but potentially internationally."

Borden was about to say something else when there was a knock on his office door. He saw through the glass that it was Detective Cross and motioned for her to enter.

Looking around Borden's office at the three guests, she said, "Detective Borden, I need to speak to you outside your office for a moment."

Borden was glad she was here. He needed time to process what these federal agents had been telling him.

"What's this about, Cross?" asked Borden. Cross hesitated, and Borden knew her predicament. "It's okay, you can speak freely."

As the three agents stood up, Borden introduced them. "Detective Cross is my partner." "These two gentlemen and lady are Sergeant Crawford and Sergeant Westwood of the RCMP and Agent Spade from CSIS."

"Sir, there has been another shooting. This one was fatal. We don't have all the facts yet, but it happened at the large country estate of a man named Bob Jackson who is a mortgage broker for one of the major banks."

"Okay, Cross, get the team ready, get the address, and be ready to roll in 5 minutes."

"If you don't mind, Detective Borden," said Sergeant Crawford, "we would like to come with you. Given what we just discussed about this group having accomplices in the banking industry, this shooting may be related to our investigation."

"Okay," Borden replied. "You three follow us and we'll regroup at the scene."

The three Feds assured Borden they would stay out of the way. This was not their case to solve. For now, they were just there as observers.

Arriving at the address of the shooting, Borden and Cross drove through a set of ornate iron gates onto the circular driveway of a well-manicured landscape. Borden stopped behind a police cruiser that was parked in front of the sprawling ranch home.

"Good day, sir. I'm Constable Jenkins. My partner and I were the first on the scene. He's inside now comforting the housekeeper, who discovered the body."

"What do we know so far, constable?"

"Upon arriving, the housekeeper escorted us to the room where the victim was shot and had fallen. After checking for vital signs, and observing the obvious gunshot wound to his head, I knew he was dead. That's when we secured the crime scene and alerted your office. I'll take you there now."

"Cross, while I follow Constable Jenkins, go question the housekeeper."

Cross found the housekeeper seated at a table in the kitchen. "Good afternoon, I'm Detective Cross and I would like to ask you a few questions. First, could you please tell me your name?"

"Yes detective, my name is Sheila."

"Thank you, Shelia. Can you tell me what happened here today?"

"I was in the main hallway cleaning the banister when I heard a breaking sound like glass falling on the floor and then a large thud in Mr. Jackson's study. I put down my cleaning cloth and rushed to the study. I knocked on the door and called out for Mr. Jackson to ask if he was okay. There was no answer.

"It was unusual for him not to acknowledge me, so I opened the door and looked inside. I saw him lying twisted on the floor with blood around his head and shoulders. Then I screamed.

"I ran back to the kitchen and called 911. They told me to remain calm, and that help was on the way."

Shelia began to sob. "What happened to Mr. Jackson? Why would anyone hurt him? He was such a kind and considerate man. He always treated me so well. He was almost like a son."

Cross put her hand on Shelia's shoulder, trying to console her. "Everything will be okay Sheila, don't worry about anything right now."

Detective Borden walked into the kitchen, and Cross introduced him to Shelia, who offered to get the detectives a cup of tea.

"That's very kind of you Shelia, but for now, I have to borrow Detective Cross from you to show her something outside."

Cross followed Borden out of the house and toward a large window on the side overlooking the backyard patio.

"As you can see, Cross, it appears from the shattered window that a bullet must have come from the treed area over there at the edge of the field.

"I want you to take the two constables with you and see if you can find any evidence the shooter might have left behind, assuming that was their staging area.

"If you find anything, wait for the Forensic Team, so they can bag it and tag it. Then quietly return here. I don't want to give the Feds any reason to mess around with our investigation."

Chapter 25

It was a glorious Sunday afternoon. Warm but not hot. Beautiful blue sky, with not a cloud to be found anywhere.

Despite the beauty all around her, Cross was anything but happy. "How much can a person take before they break?" she wondered. The last two and a half days were, as they say, "one for the books." Two people had been shot; one was dead. There was the booby-trapped house, an exploding SUV, and her boss falling from a ladder and banging his head hard enough that he probably had a concussion. And to add insult to injury, three federal agents were now watching their every move.

She nonchalantly approached Constable Jenkins so that nothing looked out of the usual. "Jenkins, unless you have something else that needs to be done, could you and your partner come with me to look for some clues on this case?"

"Certainly, Detective Cross."

"Borden figures the shooter was positioned in that treed area across the field, and he wants us to check it out. We need to keep this between us. Three Feds are snooping around, and we don't need them interfering in this case right now. Are you two good with that? What we find is between the three of us, and Detective Borden, of course."

"Okay, Detective. we are with you!" replied Jenkins. His partner nodded his agreement.

Hopping into Jenkins' cruiser, the three of them headed out of the driveway and drove down the road in the direction of the wooded area.

"Look ahead on the right," Jenkins said. "There's an overgrown driveway that looks like it might be an entrance to those trees." He stopped in front of the driveway.

As they got out of the car, Cross pointed. "Look over there. It appears as if some branches are broken off that tree, which could have happened if someone drove up here. Any vehicle driven up here would be hidden and nobody would see it from the road. It would be a perfect place for a shooter to set up."

As they all began walking vigilantly up the driveway toward the trees, Jenkins spotted tire tread marks. Following the tire marks to where they ended, Cross noticed something that seemed out of place. Crouching down to get a closer look, she saw what appeared to be a cigarette butt in the grass.

"Jenkins, go back to the cruiser and get some flags from your evidence kit to mark this location so the Forensic Team can easily find it. If this was from the shooter, he's not that bright. Leaving a butt for possible

DNA matching or a fingerprint has got to be one of the stupidest things he could have done."

Continuing into the woods, they carefully approached the edge that opened to an expansive field. Cross noticed an area where the grass was flattened by something or somebody that was heavy. She looked toward the house and saw that they were directly facing the side where Jackson had been shot.

"This would be a perfect spot for the shooter to set up." Even as Cross spoke the words, she knew it was all circumstantial. What they still needed was evidence to prove it.

Pulling out her cell phone, she called Borden to give him an update.

"Good work, Cross. I'll send the Forensic Team over there as soon as they finish processing the scene here at the house. Stay put and secure the scene until they arrive."

While waiting for the Forensic Team, Cross and the two constables continued examining the area looking for more evidence. Cross was scouring through underbrush when she looked up to see two young boys walking through the woods toward her.

"Hey," said the taller boy. "Are you guys looking for the man with the rifle?"

Cross turned and faced the boys, stunned by what she had just heard. "Yes," she said. "Did you see him?"

"Yup," the older boy replied. "There were two of them. One was driving the car, and the other had a rifle. They didn't see us. We were quiet and just watched them. They weren't here too long. I thought maybe they were here hunting for geese."

"How many times did he shoot the rifle?" Cross asked, barely able to suppress a laugh at her good fortune.

"He only shot once, and then he jumped to his feet so fast he smacked his head on that big dead tree branch. Then he started swearing and yelling at the other guy to hurry up."

Chiming in, the other boy said, "That's when the other guy picked up the blanket off the ground, while the guy with the rifle took it apart and stuffed all the pieces in a big black bag. They both ran real fast to get to their car."

"Did either of you boys notice the licence plate on the car?"

"Yes, I saw the licence plate. Do you want the number?" asked the older boy.

"That would be very helpful, young man," Cross replied as she took out her notepad and pen to write it down.

"One more thing. You said he had a blanket on the ground."

"Yes ma'am. It was like a blanket or maybe a big towel like the ones my mom uses when we go to the beach. It was bright orange. He placed it on the ground right over there. He got down on it when he was shooting his rifle. I guess he didn't want to get dirty."

Trying to be the professional she was, Cross fought to maintain a straight face. This information would blow the case wide open. "What are your names, boys?"

"I'm Billy Jamison," said the older boy. "This is my friend Jack Boyle."

"Hi, Billy. Hello Jack. My name is Detective Cross. Do you boys live around here?"

"Yes," replied Billy. "We go hiking through here all the time."

"Do you boys know the man who lives in the big house across this field?"

"Sure, that's Mr. Jackson's house. He is nice to us, and he doesn't mind if we hike around here," said Billy.

The sky was now darkening, and Cross didn't even care that this would be another late night or maybe early morning before she could get to bed. All she could think of was this huge break that had fallen into her lap. "You mentioned that you live in this area. How far away from here do you live?"

"Oh, my house is not far from here. It's about a mile down the road that way," Billy said. "Jack lives right beside me. We're best friends." Cross wrote down the names of their parents, addresses, and phone numbers.

"Billy, if I showed you pictures of some men, do you think you and Jack could tell which ones were out here with the rifle and the car?"

"Yup, we could do that. We got a really good look at them, didn't we, Jack?" Jack was speechless, but he managed a brief nod.

"So, Billy and Jack, are you sure these men didn't see or hear you?"

"I don't think so, replied Jack. Am I right, Billy?" It was Billy's turn to nod.

"Now, this is important, boys, so listen carefully. If you want to help us, don't talk to anybody else about what happened here today. Please don't say anything to your friends at school either, okay?" We want to be sure that these men don't find out that you saw them."

Chapter 26

It was 6:00 a.m. as Borden quietly got out of bed. The weekend had come and gone, and he was nowhere closer to being on vacation. Seeing that his wife Lois was still sleeping soundly, his heart filled with gratitude. "She has always been my rock," he thought. "Even with all these years of late nights, early mornings, and missed anniversaries, she has never complained."

He wondered how much longer she could put up with this and how much longer he could continue sacrificing his own family for a job that was becoming more stressful by the day and somewhat meaningless. When you arrest one bad guy, he's immediately replaced by three more. And the one bad guy you catch often gets away with a reprimand.

Arriving at the office early, Borden was happy to see that Cross was already sitting at her desk.

"Forensics handed me this report just after I got here this morning, Borden. The evidence they collected at the shooting location in the woods yesterday ties the murder of Bob Jackson with Carson Blocker's shooting four days ago at Complete Real Estate. It's the Temple brothers.

"The blood and skin fragments on the dead tree branch that the boys pointed out to me match Stan Temple's DNA, which means he was the shooter, and his brother Derek is the careless smoker who left his cigarette butt on the ground. There is no word yet on the alert we issued last night to all local law enforcement with the licence plate number and make and model of their car that we got from the database."

"That's great news, Cross! I couldn't think of a better way to start my day. That was wonderful work you did out there yesterday."

Borden envied Cross and, at the same time, felt sorry for her. She was well on her way to becoming the youngest Chief of Police in record time. He knew that was her goal, but he also knew it would come with a consequence. "Cross probably doesn't realize what she'll have to give up to get what she wants," he mused. "She'll spend even less time with her husband Bill than she does now, and they'll probably never know the joy of having children."

Snapping his thoughts back to the tasks at hand, Borden decided that the priority for this morning was to interview Carson Blocker at the hospital. The doctors had finally given the go-ahead for a visit, being satisfied that his brain injury was healing.

After a 20-minute drive to the hospital, Borden and Cross found their way to Carson Blocker's private room. After introducing themselves, Borden asked questions while Cross took notes.

"Are you feeling well enough to answer a few questions for us, Carson?"

"No problem detective. My shoulder is sore, and I still have a headache, but my memory is getting better each day, and I'm feeling stronger."

"What can you tell us about the night you were shot?"

"I don't remember much about it. The only thing I recall is working late to get some transactions approved. It was just after 3:00 a.m. when I finished, and I went to the men's room before heading home. When I came back to my office, I saw someone dressed all in black with a ski mask over his face trying to steal my computer. I yelled at him, and I think we started fighting with each other."

"Carson, do you remember how many shots were fired?"

"I don't know for sure. I felt a sudden pain in my shoulder. It all happened so fast, and then I guess I fell and hit my head."

"The good news, Carson, is that over the past few days, we've been able to identify the two men who assaulted you. We're currently investigating the possibility that these two men are tied to an organized crime group that specializes in identity theft and fraud. We believe they took your computers to access the personal information of all your high-wealth clients. And we believe that they broke into your office that night because their original plan to get that information failed."

"Do you know what their original plan was?"

Borden didn't want to burden Carson yet with the details about Andrea Talbot. "That's part of an ongoing investigation that we can't talk about right now. I promise I'll fill you in on all the details when the time is right."

Carson seemed satisfied with Borden's response.

"You should also know that your home was broken into. Your laptop, and the one belonging to your wife, was stolen."

"Is Chelsea all right? Did they hurt her too?"

"Your wife wasn't home at the time. She's fine except for being worried sick about what happened to you."

For a moment, Carson was stunned and lost for words. Then in a soft voice, he stuttered, "If anything had happened to Chelsea, I could never forgive myself."

"Why do you say that, Carson?"

"Because she's been very upset lately that I've been putting my work first, and that it's ruining our marriage. My work might have gotten her shot just like me if she was home when they broke in. Oh no, what have I done?"

Sensing that this was all the news that Carson could take for one day in his current condition, Borden and Cross said their goodbyes. On their way to the elevator, they both saw Chelsea sitting patiently in the waiting room.

"Detectives, the doctor called me this morning and said I could see my husband as soon as you finished questioning him about the shooting. Is he okay? Can I see him now?"

Cross smiled and looked deep into Chelsea's eyes. "He's doing just fine Chelsea. And, I have a hunch that your visit with him right now is going to be just what the doctor ordered."

Chapter 27

As Borden and Cross were driving back to the office from the hospital, their conversation about the case was interrupted by a dispatcher on the police radio. "Detective Borden, we have a hit on the BOLO that was issued after the Jackson shooting. I'm patching you into Constable Clark for an update."

"Hello, Clark, this is Detective Borden. I'm here with Detective Cross. What can you tell us?"

"Hello, detectives. I was patrolling in the Beaches area when I spotted a car with the license plate number listed in the be-on-the-lookout bulletin. The vehicle was stopped at a red light, and I had a clear view of the driver and passenger. They look identical to the pictures of Stan and Derek Temple in the bulletin.

"I'm driving a ghost car, so I followed them at a safe distance. They parked in the driveway of a small house on Beech Avenue and went directly inside. I have the house under surveillance right now."

"Good work Clark. I'm going to contact the Emergency Task Force now and coordinate with them to determine the best staging area for us to meet before we swarm the house. Let us know if anything changes before we get there."

The drive to the Beaches area went fast as Borden continued to coordinate plans for the operation with the Emergency Task Force, the Toronto Police Services version of SWAT.

When they arrived at the staging area in a parking lot about one block from the house where Stan and Derek were located, Borden assembled the tactical team for a briefing on the operation at hand.

"Stan and Derek Temple should be considered armed and dangerous. The last time we tried to apprehend these two suspects there was a hailstorm of gunfire and explosions. If they've booby-trapped this house the same way, there will be a danger to all the surrounding residents.

"Job one is to evacuate anyone who lives close for safety's sake and for Detective Cross to do some up-close recon, so we know what to expect when we storm the house.

"Job two is to make sure these two don't slip through our fingers again. You all know your assignments. Take up your positions and wait for my command to engage."

Detective Cross removed any clothing that identified her as the police and placed her gun in the small of her back under her shirt. She put her badge into her pocket and pulled her hair down to hide the two-way communication device in her ear that connected her to the entire team on a secure channel.

Two plainclothes policewomen were doing the same thing. They each grabbed a clipboard, some flyers, and business cards for a fake company from the tactical van that was serving as the command center. Anyone noticing the three women walking door-to-door would easily believe they were conducting a survey in the neighborhood.

Starting two properties away from the target house, Cross ambled up the front walkway and onto the front porch. She knocked on the door and waited.

An elderly lady peered out the front window, and after giving Cross a sharp look over, decided it was safe to open her door. "Yes, young lady. What can I do for you?"

"Good morning, Ma'am, I'm surveying the neighborhood to determine which houses have Fiber Optic Internet service."

"Oh no, we don't have any Internet service of any kind. We don't see any need for the Internet, thank you." She was about to close the door when Cross took her badge out of her pocket.

"Ma'am, I'm with the police, and we're conducting an investigation pertaining to one of your neighbors." Flipping to the last page on her clipboard, she produced pictures of Stan and Derek.

"Have you seen either of these two men in the neighborhood?"

By now, the lady had fully opened her door and was carefully looking at the pictures of Stan and Derek.

"Yes, they look like the two men that live in the house two doors down the street from here, but I can't be sure. They don't seem to be around here all that much."

"Thank you so much for that information. Just a few more questions. Do they have children or anyone else living in the house that you know of?"

"No, I don't believe so. I haven't seen anyone else living there. They keep pretty much to themselves."

"That's good Ma'am. Is there anyone else with you in the house right now?"

"Just my husband. He's watching TV."

"Okay, when I leave, I need you and your husband to wait for a minute and then go for a walk. When you come out of your house, turn to the right and walk up to Queen Street."

Cross took a card out of her breast pocket. "Please don't come back for at least one hour. Before you come back, call the number on the back of this card to make sure it's safe. Can you do that for me? Will that be a problem?"

"No problem. We can do that."

"Thank you, and have a nice day, Ma'am."

"You be careful young lady."

Cross turned and casually walked down the driveway to the sidewalk, and then to the house next to the one belonging to Stan and Derek.

She went through the same routine with the young man who answered the door. After studying the photos, he told Cross that the two men had only been at the house a few times during the past month. As far as he knew, they were the only ones who lived there. He assured her that he would leave within five minutes to go to work and would not return before calling to make sure it was safe.

While Cross had been knocking on doors, the policewomen had been doing the same across the street and on the other side of the house occupied by their two suspects.

Cross could hear Borden's voice in her earpiece, "Are you sure you feel comfortable doing this, Cross? It is risky."

"I know, Borden, but if Stan or Derek saw us knocking on doors in the neighborhood and we don't knock on their door, they might become suspicious."

Without hesitation, Cross walked up to the front door and boldly knocked.

Chapter 28

Seconds passed that seemed like minutes before Cross decided to knock again much harder than before. This time she could hear footsteps across a hardwood floor coming toward her.

Opening the door, a sour-looking Derek Temple snarled, "What do you want?" Then he realized he was looking at a pretty lady, and his face softened with a smile that made Cross want to throw up.

"Excuse me, sir, we are conducting a survey to determine how many people in the neighborhood are using Fiber Optic Internet. Do you use Fiber Optic for your Internet service or regular high-speed Internet?"

"We don't use Fiber Optic, only high speed," Derek replied. He could hear Stan in the background telling him to shoo the saleslady away. Stan had been watching her knocking on the doors of other houses, and whatever she was selling, he didn't want.

But it had been a long time since Derek had spoken to anyone other than Stan, and he was enjoying his conversation with Cross.

"Does anyone besides you and your wife use the Internet here?" Cross asked.

"I'm not married. I live here with my brother," replied Derek.

"So, there's only the two of you on the Internet?"

"That's correct."

"Do you have unlimited Internet usage at the maximum speed?" Cross asked.

Derek glanced sideways to see Stan in the living room, drawing his fingers across his throat. It was time to shut this conversation down.

"I hate to be rude, but I have to go now."

"Okay then, I'm sorry to have bothered you," replied Cross.

Pulling a phony promotional flyer from her clipboard, she handed it to Derek.

"If you ever decide to switch to Fiber Optic, sir, please call us at the number on this flyer. We have a special price for the rest of this month."

As Derek closed the door, Cross deliberately dropped her pen and bent down to pick it up so she could put her ear close to the lock. She didn't hear the deadbolt being engaged. "Yes!" she thought. "This will make for a quick entrance."

Walking casually back up the street and out of view, Cross entered an unmarked police car and headed back to the staging area to join the final preparations for the raid.

The plan was for two ETF teams to enter the front and rear of the house at the same time. Uniformed police would hide in strategic positions around the house to prevent Stan and Derek from making a hasty exit through windows or on motorcycles from any hidden tunnel as they had done a few days before.

The teams synced their communication pieces and headed out in full stealth mode to take up their positions. Seeing that everyone was in place, Borden spoke quietly into his communication device, "Everyone move on my three. One. Two. Three."

With the front door unlocked, the ETF team positioned there was the first to enter, closely followed by Borden, Cross, and two uniformed constables. Although the back door was locked, the team at the rear of the house broke through it in seconds.

Derek was lying on the couch listening to music on his headphones. The music was so loud he didn't hear the police barge in. Seeing the ETF officers rushing toward him, he jumped to his feet, but there was nowhere to run. One constable grabbed him while another handcuffed his hands behind his back.

Stan came running out of an upstairs bedroom with his handgun at the ready. Looking down from the top of the stairs, he counted four rifles pointing directly at him.

"The house is surrounded. There is no escape. Put down your weapon, now!" barked the ETF team leader.

Every fiber of Stan's being wanted to go out shooting as he had seen in the movies. But, after staring down the barrels of all those rifles for a few more seconds, he decided he would rather live to fight another day.

Chapter 29

A uniformed constable escorted Derek into the small interrogation room. Detective Cross remained behind the one-way mirror while Borden went in to meet with Derek.

As Detective Borden entered, he asked Derek if he would like a coffee or some water. Derek declined both.

"Derek, I want to be honest with you. Based on the information we have, you are in a heap of trouble. If you cooperate and tell us what we want to know, this could help you at your trial.

"At this very moment, your brother is being offered the same opportunity, and one of you will tell us what we want to know. The first one to speak up and answer our questions is the one who will benefit.

"Once that happens, there will be no deals of any kind for the other person. Do you understand?"

"I didn't do anything," said Derek.

"Derek, you are looking at a lengthy prison term, and you will probably never see your brother again because you will go to different prisons. You need to start looking out for yourself. Nobody is going to help you, but I can if you cooperate with me.

"Tell me, why is your hand bruised and your knuckles healing? Were you in a fight with someone recently?"

"I wasn't in a fight. You're trying to set me up. I don't know what you're talking about."

"Okay, then what were you doing with the drugs we found in the house? Were you going to sell them?"

"I don't know anything about any drugs. I have some Tylenol, nothing else."

"Then I guess those drugs belong to your brother. I'll charge him with possession for the purpose of selling narcotics and name you as an accessory to drug trafficking. How does that sound to you?"

"Stan has done nothing wrong, and I have done nothing. You need to let us go and stop making stuff up."

It surprised Borden that Derek hadn't asked to see a lawyer, but then again, Derek didn't seem to be that smart.

"Forget the drugs for a minute, tell me what you were doing at the offices of Complete Real Estate in the early hours of Friday morning."

"I don't know what you're talking about. I've never heard of that place. You're just trying to confuse me."

"Okay, have it your way, Derek. But if the person you shot at the real estate office dies, you'll be charged with murder. And then, the drugs won't matter because you'll end up dying in prison."

"You're crazy man. I didn't shoot anyone."

"Well, then," Borden pressed, "I guess it was your brother who did the shooting. Is that how it was Derek?"

"My brother didn't shoot anyone."

Borden paused briefly to watch Derek squirm in his seat. "So, what did you do today, Derek?"

"I spent most of the day watching television."

"Did you watch it at your house in The Beaches, Derek?"

"Yeah, I did."

"What programs did you watch?"

"I don't know. Different stuff you know. I don't remember the names of programs."

"Derek, here's the problem. You say you were watching television, but there is no television in the house where you were arrested. Or should I say, there is a television, but it isn't working?

"So, why don't you start telling me the truth? Help me out here and I might be able to help you because you are heading to prison for an awfully long time. You will probably die in prison. Hey, but at least you'll get an hour of fresh air each day when they let you walk in the yard."

Borden could see that Derek was becoming more agitated. He thought just a few more questions would be all he needed to tip him over the edge.

"Derek, you are running out of time. Remember we are talking to Stan right now and the first one who helps us will get a sweet deal. This is your last chance, then your get-out-of-jail-free card will disappear forever.

You understand the meaning of the word 'forever,' don't you?"

"I haven't done anything wrong. You've got the wrong man. You need to let me and my brother go!"

Borden opened a file folder he had brought into the room. "Derek, we have a video of you driving an SUV from the garage of the Complete Real Estate office, where you fought with and shot one of their employees."

"There's no way you have a video of that. I cut the video feed to all the cameras in the garage."

"You just admitted to being there. Now we're getting somewhere. We also have two witnesses who saw you and your brother murder Bob Jackson. We have DNA evidence that places you at the scene of the shooting. You might want to stop smoking before you find your-self at another crime scene. That's right Derek, you left a cigarette butt behind. Not very smart."

Borden could see the wheels turning inside Derek's head as he tried to think about the last time he had a smoke.

"Should I go on, Derek? How am I doing so far, Derek?

"Did I mention that we recovered the murder weapon and the orange beach towel used at that shooting from our raid on your house today?

"So, do you really think I'm going to believe your story that you haven't done anything wrong?"

Derek stared blankly at Borden and said nothing.

After a few more seconds of silence, Borden rose to his feet and headed for the door.

"It's been nice chatting with you, Derek. I'll see you in about 30 or maybe 35 years from now when they release you from Penetanguishene penitentiary. I'm going to see if your brother has decided to take our deal."

As Borden reached for the doorknob, Derek cried out, "Wait! What kind of deal can you give me?"

"That depends on how much you help me, Derek. Let's start by you telling me about the shooting at the real estate office."

"I didn't shoot anyone. Stan was the one who did the shooting. He didn't want to, but he had no choice. The guy was about to split my head open with a golf trophy. Stan did it to save me."

"Why did you and Stan break into the office?"

"A woman was supposed to give us a flash drive with information on it, but she refused at the last minute. So, we broke in to steal some computers to get the information we needed."

"What information was supposed to be on the flash drive, Derek?"

"I don't know. Honestly, you've got to believe me, detective."

"Oh sure, I have to believe you. Okay Derek, if you want to start telling me the truth now, who told you and Stan to get this information?"

"All I know is it that everyone calls him Madler. I don't know his first name. I've never even seen the guy. He always contacts Stan directly with instructions."

"What kind of instructions does he normally give Stan?"

"It's mostly the same stuff. He tells Stan what real estate office to get information from and a person on the inside to threaten so they'll give us a flash drive. If we don't get the flash drive, we break in to get the computers. Then we hand off the information to one of Madler's guys wherever he tells us to meet him."

"How long have you and your brother been doing this for Madler?"

"I don't know. It's been maybe three years. We started working for him in British Columbia, and then we moved to Alberta, and now we're here in Ontario."

Borden was starting to wonder if he was hearing the truth. He had never seen anyone disclose information so fast in all his years in police work. He couldn't figure out why Derek broke so quickly.

"Go on, Derek, you're doing great. Now tell me about the Bob Jackson shooting. Who told you to kill him?"

"It was Madler. He told Stan to shoot Jackson. I didn't want any part of it. I never wanted anyone to ever get hurt. I begged Stan not to shoot him and to just walk away. I told him we could get lost somewhere in Australia or South America, but he said the Cartel would track us down and kill us. He said we had to keep following Madler's orders or we would die."

Chapter 30

After a few more minutes of questioning Derek, Borden knew he had heard enough. Joining Cross in the room behind the one-way mirror, he said, "It looks like our hunch about the escape tunnel at Stan and Derek's safe house being Cartel 101 was correct. The Cartel is somehow involved in all of this."

Cross nodded in agreement. "It's obvious that Derek doesn't know the details, but I'm betting that Stan does. But I have a feeling he won't sing as fast as his brother did."

"It's nothing you can't handle, Cross. I'll sit this one out. It will give me time to bring the RCMP and CSIS into the loop about what we've learned so far."

A few minutes later, Cross entered the interrogation room and sat opposite Stan. She purposefully placed a cup of coffee in front of him. "Double, double, Stan, just the way you like it."

"You think you know everything about me?" Stan shot back. "Well, you don't know anything!" Then he reached for the coffee and took a sip.

"Just so you know Stan, Derek is being questioned right now in another room. The way things stand, from what we already know, you are looking at 25 to 35 years in prison, along with your brother. But things will become a lot better for the first person who answers our questions."

Cross paused to allow this to sink in and then continued.

"At this point, we've pieced together most of what happened over the last four days. You and your brother have been busy little campers, haven't you?"

Stan took another drink of his coffee. "I don't know what you're talking about. I've done nothing wrong. You have the wrong guy."

"Who shot the person at the Complete Real Estate office, Stan?"

"What real estate office?" muttered Stan as he stared at his coffee cup on the table.

"So, help me understand, you weren't at any real estate office four days ago?"

"That's right, cop. I don't know what you're talking about."

"Who told you to shoot the person at the real estate office?"

"I told you, cop lady, I don't know anything about real estate offices or any shooting."

"Are you sure about that?"

Stan glared at Cross and sneered, "Yeah, I'm sure about that."

"Just so you know Stan, we're examining the gun that you were waving around at your house today to see if it's the same gun used at the office shooting. If we find a match, you'll be in deep trouble Stan, and I won't be able to help you at all unless you cooperate now."

Stan was suddenly silent. Cross could sense that he was frantically thinking about his next move.

"Are you hearing me, Stan? Do you understand what I'm saying?"

"Yeah, I hear you. Now you hear me. I didn't do anything, got it? I've done nothing wrong. Sure, I was waving a gun. I have the right to defend myself when someone breaks into my home don't I? Maybe I should call a lawyer. Do I need a lawyer?"

"That's up to you, Stan. But the evidence we already have is stacked against you. We know you were the shooter in the Bob Jackson murder."

"Never heard of the guy. You're just trying to trick me."

"Wrong answer, Stan. We have two eyewitnesses to you firing a rifle at Bob Jackson's window and then whacking the top of your head on a dead tree branch. We've already matched the blood and skin fragments we found on the branch to your DNA. You can lie all you want, Stan, but DNA doesn't lie.

"And what are the chances that ballistics will match the bullet that killed Bob Jackson to the rifle we found in your home today? So, let's stop playing games and you tell me who hired you unless you want to spend the rest of your life in federal prison."

Cross saw beads of sweat forming on Stan's forehead. "Have you ever been in federal prison, Stan? It's not a pleasant place. But somebody in there will surely take a liking to you.

"Oh, and as for Derek, he will get a deal for cooperating with us in our investigation. Derek will be free before you know it. By the time you get out of prison, if you do, you'll have nephews and nieces who are as old as you are right now.

"Last chance Stan. Who was it that hired you?"

"Derek knows who it is, I don't remember his name."

"Bye Stan, see you in thirty-five years. Come by and say hello."

Cross closed her file, pushed her chair back from the table, and stood up to leave.

"His name is Madler," shot back Stan. "It's Madler. He's behind all of this."

Cross returned to her chair and sat down. "Don't waste my time, Stan. If you lie to me once more, I'm gone for good and so are you. Now tell me, who is Madler? Does Madler have a first name?"

"He never uses his first name. Everyone just calls him Madler."

"Have you ever met with him in person?"

"Yeah, when he first recruited me and Derek in Vancouver. I saw him again in Calgary, and once here in Toronto. Most of the time he communicates with me on burner phones."

"Where did you meet him in those places, Stan?"

"It was always in a hotel room. He likes living in hotels because there's no commitment involving a lease and stuff like that. And he can pick up and leave at a moment's notice if he has to."

"What hotel did you see him at here in Toronto?"

"It was the Four Seasons, but he checked out of there right after meeting with me, so I wouldn't know where to find him again."

"You're doing good, Stan. Keep talking and you might get to see Derek's kids if he ever has any. Tell me about the tunnel you and your brother used to escape from your safe house, the one that has Cartel written all over it."

Stan was caught off guard by the question and quickly realized that this cop knew a lot more about the operation than he thought she did.

"Madler bought the house and told us to build the tunnel a couple of months ago. He said his new part- ners wanted things done their way. He sent over some Mexicans disguised as excavation contractors to help us. When the neighbors asked what we were doing, we told them we were building a root cellar."

"Did Madler say who his partners were? Did he tell you they were Cartel?"

Stan went silent for a minute, and Cross could see fear in his eyes as he began to speak, "If I tell you everything I know, can you promise to give me and my brother pro- tection? Can you put us in a witness protection program or something like that so Madler and Juan Estrada can never find us?"

"Who's Juan? Is he Cartel, Stan?"

"Yeah, and from everything I've heard he doesn't tolerate loose ends. Neither does Madler. Now that we've been arrested, we're as good as dead if you don't protect us."

"The best way for us to protect you and your brother is to find and arrest both Madler and Juan, and the sooner the better. Once they're in custody, we can make sure your paths never cross again. So, tell me everything you know, Stan."

Chapter 31

Carson was excited to be going home, although 'excited' was perhaps too weak a word for someone who had narrowly escaped death. The doctor had told him that he would have bled out hours before he was found if the bullet had hit the major artery just one inch higher in his shoulder.

"Doug, you didn't have to cut your vacation short to come back just because I got shot. You should have stayed in Hawaii and enjoyed a little rest and relaxation."

"Carson, how could I rest and relax knowing that my best friend was lying in a hospital bed because I had convinced him to come to Toronto and work with me?"

"Well, I appreciate you being here, and thanks for picking me up at the hospital to drive me home. It will save Chelsea from making the trip in rush hour traffic to come and get me."

"I'm so happy to hear that you and Chelsea are back together!"

"Yes, the shooting has changed the way be both look at our relationship. All Chelsea wants is for me to be a bigger part of her life than my job. I'm really starting to second guess why I've been working so hard to get ahead, and not taking the time to focus on the things and the people, like Chelsea, that really matter."

"Hey, I'm happy to give you some time off if that's what you need to patch things up with Chelsea."

"Thanks, Doug, that would be great. But I'm going to need a lot of time off for another reason. The doctors told me that the bullet wound will heal nicely and, with a program of physiotherapy for the next four weeks, I should be as good as new to win some money from you on the golf course again.

"But the bigger problem is my brain injury. He said that when I hit my head after being shot, I was unconscious for much longer than normal because of the point of impact and the force of the blow. He says I have a brain injury that's going to take about six months to completely heal. His recommendation is to take the next eight weeks off and do nothing that causes me stress."

"Carson, that's no problem. Take all the time you need. But there's no way you're winning money from me on the golf course!" Doug chuckled.

"I'm glad you're okay with this. Chelsea and I were thinking of taking a trip back home. I've already talked to my brother Luke, and he and Melissa would be happy to have us stay with them for as long as I need to recuperate."

"Go for it, buddy. I'll be happy to handle your outstanding deals while you're away, so you have nothing to worry about. When are you thinking of leaving?"

"Now that I know you're okay with this, I'm going to book a flight for Chelsea and me first thing tomorrow morning."

As Doug maneuvered his car slowly through traffic amidst the honking horns of impatient drivers, Carson noticed a park straight ahead and to the right of the roadway. It was a tiny patch of green that looked out of place in Toronto, but just the kind of thing many people wouldn't even pay attention to in Alberta.

"Tell me, Doug, do you ever miss living out west and our dreams of owning a golf course?"

Keeping his eyes on the road but glancing at Carson, Doug smiled as he spoke, "You saw that park back there, didn't you? A little touch of sanity in a world gone mad. Yes, Carson, I have thought of that golf course many times and I hope that someday we'll be able to build it."

"You know, Doug, getting shot has changed my perspective quite a bit. For some time, I haven't been enjoying life in the big city all that much. I miss the family ranch, the horses, the Chinook winds, camping out, and our climbs up Mount Norquay. Would you ever consider moving back?"

"Yes. I'm sure a day will come when that all makes sense, but now that I own a real estate company, I can't imagine that's going to happen any time soon."

"What would it take, Doug, for you to move back to Canmore and pursue our dream of becoming CPGA pros and owning our own golf course?"

Doug was silent for a few moments. Carson was his friend, and he didn't want to crush his dreams. But Doug also realized that they were still his dreams too. In a perfect world, what he really wanted was what Carson wanted. "I'd need to see the perfect opportunity. I'd need to know that the success I was giving up in Toronto would be equal to or greater than the success I could have by pursuing our dream."

Carson smiled, "So, you're saying there's a chance we could still do this?"

"I'll tell you what. If you ever find the perfect opportunity, just pick up the phone and tell me it's time to come home. I'll figure out how to make that happen. That's a promise."

"Sounds good to me, my friend. I'm going to hold you to that promise."

For the next few minutes, they discussed how to manage things at the office for Carson's clients while he was gone, and the need for Andrea Talbot to become involved popped up. Not knowing what Doug already knew, Carson sensed he needed to tread lightly with his next question. "So how is Andrea doing?"

"Detective Borden told me everything that happened. It was incredibly brave of her not to give up the thumb drive to the guys who broke into the office and shot you. Given her cooperation, and her circumstances, the police have decided not to press charges."

"Are you okay with her continuing to be my assistant?"

"Absolutely! The bravery and the loyalty she showed to us and to our clients is one in a million. I've given her the rest of the week off. She and her daughter are safely back at home now that the two men who threatened her and shot you are in police custody."

Chapter 32

Borden and Cross had spent the last two hours in his office pouring over all the details that Derek and Stan had provided in their interrogation. As soon as Borden had heard that Madler preferred to stay in hotels, he mobilized a team of detectives, including Kim and Friedman, to begin contacting every hotel in the Toronto area for a guest with the last name of Madler.

"Cross, it's only a matter of time before we track Madler down. We can assume he's still staying in the Toronto area, because Stan told us the Mexicans who helped him build the escape tunnel were working for Madler in a warehouse. The workers didn't know where the warehouse was because they were driven there each day in a windowless van. But they knew it took about 30 minutes to get there from where they were picked up each morning in the city."

"I agree, boss. And because these workers said they were packaging drugs from Mexico, we can assume that's the Cartel connection. It's a good thing for us that the Mexicans took a liking to Stan and told him so much."

"Sergeant Crawford at the RCMP and Danielle Spade of CSIS have assured me that they will provide whatever backup support we need to find the location of that warehouse and—"

Before he could finish his thought, Detective Friedman came bursting through the door of Borden's office. "Boss, I found him! There is a Jason Madler registered as a guest at the Ford Hotel. He checked in two weeks ago and is still there."

"Well done, Friedman! Let the other detectives know and tell them to stand by. We'll all be heading to the hotel before the dinner hour."

Tuning to Cross, Borden continued, "I want you to assemble a team to stake out the hotel and figure out how to track every move Madler makes."

"Boss, if you have no objection, I'd like Constable Gibson to be part of this team. He's smart and eager to help. I think he has detective potential, and this could be an opportunity for him to prove it."

Both Borden and Cross were impressed with Gibson's work. He had a boyish face that looked more like a computer geek than a police constable. They decided that Gibson should be the one to approach the front desk to inquire about Madler.

A few hours later, Constable Gibson entered the lobby of the hotel in plain clothes and looked around to see who was there. The lobby was empty except for the odd person leaving the dining room or coming off an elevator.

Gibson approached the front desk and identified himself, showing the clerk his badge. "Don't refer to me as a police constable," Gibson whispered. "Just call me Mr. Gibson."

He asked the front desk clerk for his name and then inquired if Jason Madler was a guest at the hotel.

"Oh yes, Mr. Gibson, the gentleman in question has been a guest here for some time. I haven't seen him recently, but I've been off work for two days."

"Do you have any video surveillance in the main lobby?" asked Gibson. "The problem is, although Mr. Madler is a person of interest to us, we don't know what he looks like."

The desk clerk confirmed they had video of the front lobby area and video cameras at the back of the hotel as well as in the elevators for the safety of their guests. "Let me introduce you to my manager. He can give you access to those video recordings."

Within minutes, the hotel manager was able to point out Jason Madler in a lobby video from a day earlier. Gibson took a copy of the video down the street to a police surveillance vehicle, cleverly disguised as a handyman's van.

Gibson stepped inside the van and handed the video to a technician who quickly grabbed a still frame that clearly showed Madler's face. Then he printed out copies for all the members of the stake-out team. Everyone now knew whom they were looking for, and the picture

was so clear and crisp it would be easy to spot him a
mile away.

Chapter 33

The team had no idea when or if Madler would return to the Ford Hotel that night, but to Borden, it made sense that he would show up sometime before midnight to catch some shuteye. But, just in case, he had Cross assemble a second stakeout shift to take over from midnight to 8:00 the next morning.

The first shift of plainclothes police took up strategic positions in and around the hotel and casually went about their business as if they belonged there. Cross and Borden stationed themselves inside the control room of the hotel, where they could watch the coming and going of everyone from all the cameras on a bank of video monitors.

Just after 7:00 in the evening, Constable Gibson could be heard loud and clear by all team members in the miniature earpieces of their communication devices. "The suspect has just exited a black Range Rover in the parking circle at the front entrance of the hotel and is heading into the lobby."

As Madler entered the hotel, several detectives dressed in clothes that spelled 'tourist' were leaving the dining room and moving into the lobby. At the same time, a detective disguised as a homeless man pretended to fall behind Madler's SUV and placed a tracking device underneath the vehicle.

Oblivious to everything happening around him, Madler approached the clerk at the front desk. "I'm just going up to my room to pack my things and I'll be down in a few minutes to check out."

"Yes, sir, and what is your room number?"

" 607"

"Is everything all right, sir?"

"Yes, everything is fine. Just have my bill ready, would you?"

"Yes sir, right away."

Madler headed quickly toward the two elevators just to the right of the hotel lobby. Pushing the 'up' button several times seemed to do nothing to hasten the elevator's arrival. Two detectives masquerading as a couple, who entered the lobby from outside just moments before, joined him at the elevators.

Turning toward Madler, the female undercover officer said, "Isn't it a pleasant evening out there tonight?"

Madler made brief eye contact and nodded in agreement.

"We just got back from dinner. We were celebrating our 20th wedding anniversary tonight."

"Happy anniversary," Madler responded with a forced smile. He was growing more impatient by the minute. When the elevator finally arrived, he dashed in, pushed the button for floor six, and waited what seemed like hours to him for the chatty couple to join him.

"We're on seven."

Madler pushed the button.

"Thank you, sir."

Madler did not respond.

Borden and Cross had a front-row seat watching all of this unfold on a monitor dedicated to the video feed from that elevator.

As soon as the door opened on the sixth floor, Madler bolted out of the elevator and stormed down the hallway toward room 607.

Unlocking the door to his room, he wasted no time gathering his belongings and stuffing them into a large suitcase.

Then he made a surgical sweep of his room, including the waste baskets, under the bed, the closet, and the room safe to be sure he left nothing behind.

Reaching into his pocket, he pulled out a burner phone and punched the pre-programmed number. Finally, hearing an answer eight rings later, he said, "Good evening, Señor Martinez. We have a problem. I've just learned that two of my men were taken into police custody earlier today, and by now they have surely been questioned."

"Do your men know who I am?"

"No, they don't even know you exist."

"But they know who you are."

"Yes, but that won't be a problem. I'm checking out of my hotel right now and heading straight to the warehouse. I'll lay low there for the next few days. This will give me time to create a new identity for myself before resuming normal operations."

"Do your men know where the warehouse is?"

"No, they have never been there. They know nothing about our operation there."

"You had better be right, Mr. Madler. Any disruption in operations at this time would not go well given the shipment that's already on its way from Mexico."

Terminating the call, Madler quickly scanned the room one last time to make sure he was leaving nothing behind before heading out the door and down the hallway. Borden and Cross watched him on the monitor as he stepped into the elevator and rode it alone to the main floor. They picked him up again on the monitor for the lobby camera as he stepped deliberately toward the front desk.

"Mr. Madler, do you want us to use your credit card that we have on file to pay your bill?"

Madler knew he couldn't risk using a credit card until he made his identity switch. "No, that's okay. I'm going to pay with cash. I was lucky at the casino in Niagara Falls last night and I want to get rid of some of this money before it burns a hole in my pocket."

The desk clerk chuckled. "No problem. I'm happy to help you save your pocket."

Leaving the hotel, Madler drove down Bay Street to Lake Shore Boulevard and up the ramp onto the Gardiner Expressway. What he didn't see in his rear-view mirror were the two unmarked police cars tailing him from a safe distance.

Chapter 34

The two surveillance units never lost sight of Madler as he made the 37-minute drive to what looked like a deserted warehouse in the northwest area of the city. Not that it mattered because the tracking device that was placed under his SUV sent precise GPS locations to everyone on the stakeout team.

Constable Gibson could see Madler exiting his SUV as he casually drove past the warehouse parking lot in the first surveillance vehicle. He continued up the road until he found a place to park that was out of sight. The second surveillance car, driven by Detective Kim, pulled off the road in an obscure spot well short of the warehouse parking lot.

Gibson radioed his location and Madler's status to all units. A few minutes later, Borden and Cross arrived and parked directly behind Kim's vehicle. At Borden's command, all remaining surveillance units were to find parking out of sight and walk to secure locations around the warehouse to take a closer look.

The first thing Borden noticed were the security cameras mounted just below the warehouse rooftop. "Heads up all units. They have a 360-degree view of the outside perimeter with video cameras. Be careful as you approach."

After just 15 minutes had passed, the sun was beginning to set, and everyone could now clearly see that all the lights were on inside the building. There were five other vehicles in the parking lot along with Madler's, so Borden knew he wasn't alone inside.

Detective Cross assigned surveillance teams to cover all four sides of the building and instructed them to report and document any activity they noticed immediately. If anyone left the building, they were to alert unmarked units that were standing by to tail them to their destination.

In the meantime, Borden contacted Brad Smith, Commander of the Emergency Task Force, to ask for his assistance in planning a raid on the warehouse. They agreed to meet at sunrise in a command vehicle to be stationed a short distance down the street and around the corner from the warehouse in an obscure location behind a vacant retail store. Borden advised Smith that he would be inviting Sergeants Crawford and Westwood of the RCMP and Danielle Spade of CSIS to be observers.

The surveillance team reported five new vehicles arriving around midnight. A man from each vehicle knocked at the main door and waited to be let inside. Shortly after, five other men exited the building and drove off in the cars that were there when Madler arrived.

When Borden and Cross arrived at the command vehicle just before 6:00 the next morning, Commander Smith was already there studying images of the warehouse and blueprints from the original construction. Borden knew the operation was in good hands. Smith was a well-seasoned veteran of several hundred similar engagements and had a track record of never losing a man.

"Here's what we know so far detectives. The warehouse appears to be occupied by at least five people around the clock who rotate on 8-hour shifts. Given that no other people have been there through the evening and overnight hours, it's likely these men are part of a security team hired to protect the drugs we suspect are inside the building. The next logical shift rotation will occur at 8:00 this morning. I recommend that we maintain surveillance until we know how many people show up during daylight hours and whether Juan Estrada will be one of them. I have three ETF teams on alert and standing by for whenever we decide to take action."

Borden nodded in agreement. "There's no point in taking down Madler without Juan. So, I guess all we can do in the meantime is play a game of wait and see."

As Smith predicted, just before 8:00, there was another shift change at the warehouse, but this time seven men arrived to replace the five who left. Minutes later, a large white van with no windows in the rear cargo area entered the parking lot and drove slowly around to the rear of the building. It pulled up directly in front of

Loading Dock #2, and the driver honked the horn once. When the door opened, the van drove inside, and the door was immediately closed.

Less than two minutes later, the van exited the building and moved out of the parking lot. A surveillance team of two vehicles began tailing it from a safe distance.

By this time, the trio of Crawford, Westwood, and Spade were also in the command vehicle observing the comings and goings outside the warehouse from the live video feed that each of the four surveillance units Cross assigned the night before was broadcasting from their locations.

"That van wasn't there long enough to load or unload cargo," said Spade. "I witnessed this same thing while I was stationed for a time in Mexico. Vans are often used to pick up workers at a pre-determined location and transport them to work so they all arrive together. Because the van has no windows in the cargo area, the workers have no clue where they are being taken, so there's no risk of them ever disclosing the location."

Acknowledging Agent Spade, Commander Smith commented, "If what you say is true, we can assume that daily drug operations are about to begin."

Not more than 10 minutes had passed before Detective Kim reported seeing two men walking back and forth in front of two upper-level windows on one side of the building. He said that no such activity had occurred during the night.

"If men are patrolling a mezzanine area, it's likely they are there to keep an eye on the workers below," said Crawford.

Westwood chimed in, "That might explain why two extra men showed up at the shift change this morning."

Borden nodded in agreement and turned to look at Smith, "What's your assault plan, Commander?"

"The first order of business will be making the ETF teams invisible to whoever is monitoring the video cameras that completely cover the outside perimeter of the warehouse.

"Next, we'll need to get a closer look at what's inside the building to determine how many people and what kind of firepower we may be up against.

"Then, we'll initiate action with disorientation tactics so that all teams can enter the building simultaneously with minimal resistance.

"Finally, we'll—"

Just then, Constable Gibson's voice could be heard in their earpieces, "A man resembling the photo of Juan Estrada we received from the Mexican police has just arrived. He is walking from his car to the main warehouse door."

After a reflective pause, Smith continued, "Ladies and gentlemen, it's showtime."

Chapter 35

Commander Smith spoke in a voice of authority, "Unit 1, we have eyes on your approach. You are good to go at your discretion."

Moments later, he could clearly see a parachute opening in the distance through his binoculars. Borden, Cross, Crawford, Westwood, and Spade were also looking skyward, tracking the path of the ETF officer as he skillfully maneuvered his parachute in their direction and touched down quietly on the flat rooftop of the warehouse.

All units could hear Smith through their communication devices as he spoke again, "Unit 1, you are clear to proceed."

Removing his parachute, the ETF officer walked softly across the roof to avoid being heard by the guards on the mezzanine level inside. Arriving at the video camera that covered the entrance to the parking lot, he removed a small electronic device from a pouch attached to his leg. Lying on his stomach and reaching down to the camera, he clipped on two wires to intercept the live video feed. He captured a still frame and set it to be the default video that would be seen on the monitor inside the warehouse.

Three ETF teams in full SWAT gear were waiting patiently in the staging area as their fellow officer repeated the same procedure for the other seven cameras that provided a 360-degree view of the outside perimeter.

"All teams move to your positions on my three. One. Two. Three. Move." Hearing Smith's command, each team of ETF officers hustled on foot into the parking lot.

One team of three officers propped a ladder up against a windowless wall and climbed to join their other team member on the roof, who was quietly cutting all around the base of the skylight for ready removal.

The second team of four headed to the metal main entry door at the side of the building. Three officers were in the ready position with rifles raised and pointed at the door, as the remaining one placed explosive charges on the hinges. Borden and Cross positioned themselves behind these men, ready to follow their lead into the building.

A final team of four moved to the two ground-level loading doors at the rear of the warehouse. While two members were placing explosive charges at strategic locations, the other two quietly inserted snake cameras under the rubber gaskets at the base of each door.

Commander Smith's voice came through loud and clear in everyone's earpiece, "Listen, all units. We now have eyes on the inside. Boxes are stacked high on skids directly in front of the first loading dock door. This should provide good cover if needed. Nothing is blocking the view from the second loading dock door. On the opposite wall, there is a mezzanine walkway. Two men armed with M4s are observing activity on the warehouse floor from that walkway.

"I count four more armed guards at each corner of the warehouse on the ground level. By my count, 12 men are working around tables at the center of the ground floor. They appear to be packaging drugs. The workers are unarmed.

"I do not see either Jason Madler or Juan Estrada. The low ceiling directly above the loading dock doors suggests there may be a mezzanine office there. Proceed on the assumption that Madler and Estrada are in that office.

"All teams report your readiness."

"Team 1, ready."

"Team 2, ready."

"Team 3, ready."

Pausing to take a deep breath, Smith gave the command, "We go on my three. One. Two. Three. Go."

One ETF officer quickly lifted the skylight that had been detached from its base. At the same time, the other threw flash-bang grenades through the opening to the warehouse floor below. As the grenades erupted, everyone inside was momentarily blinded and deafened by brilliant flashes of light and thunderous booms.

At the sound of the flash-bangs, the other two ETF officers who had positioned themselves above the upper-level windows swung down on ropes from the rooftop and crashed through the glass, landing feet first on the mezzanine walkway. The two guards stationed there were disoriented and too slow to react. A couple of shots they managed to get off lacked direction, and they were quickly subdued and put in restraints.

In time with the flash-bangs, the other two teams blew the doors open and stormed inside with rifle scopes to their eyes, ready to find their targets.

All the workers had ducked for cover beneath the tables and were lying flat on the floor. By this time, the armed guards had staggered back to their feet and were firing aimlessly in the direction of the loading dock.

From shielded positions behind the skids of boxes in front of the first loading dock door, ETF officers wounded and disabled the two guards at floor level beneath the mezzanine walkway on the opposite wall.

As Borden and Cross followed the ETF team through the main entry door, they were met by a hail of gunfire from a guard they hadn't seen in their earlier video surveillance. Cross and one ETF officer took direct hits to the chest and fell backward from the impact.

Borden instinctively fired in the direction of the shooter wounding him in the leg. It was all the time he needed to drag Cross to safety behind a skid of boxes.

Two other ETF officers ducked behind another stack of boxes and laid down cover fire while a third pulled his fallen partner behind some wooden crates.

As bullets began pummeling the boxes of drugs that were shielding them, Borden yelled to make himself heard above the racket, "Cross, are you okay?"

Cross nodded and pointed to the bullet stuck in her vest.

Meanwhile, the two ETF officers on the mezzanine walkway were taking aim at each of the armed guards on the loading dock side that were preventing the team from advancing forward. With precision marksmanship, they disabled both shooters with wounds to their arms. Hearing the all-clear in their earpieces, the four members of Team 2 immediately fanned out to cover each corner of the warehouse.

Seeing this new wave of police momentarily distracted the lone guard who still had Team 1 and Cross and Borden pinned down. The brief moment that he stopped firing his M4 was all the time needed for the Team-1 leader to get eyes on the shooter and bring him down with a short burst. Another team member rushed to put the man in restraints before he could attempt any more heroics.

The only gunfire now was coming from above. Borden stepped out from behind the boxes and looked up to see Juan and Madler popping in and out of the mezzanine office doorway to take shots at any police trying to advance up the stairway. Just then, he could hear the Team-2 leader command his squad to shoot out the interior glass windows of the office.

Seconds later, all windows shattered under a hail of bullets. Juan and Madler dove for cover behind desks, but not in time to protect themselves from the wave of glass shards that flew through the room.

Madler felt cuts to his torso and looked down to see blood oozing through his shirt. Juan had two cuts to his face streaming blood down his forehead and right cheek.

A flash-bang came flying into the room as four ETF officers bounded up the stairs and burst into the office with rifles at the ready.

"Drop your weapons! Put your hands in the air!" yelled one officer.

"Do it now!" commanded another.

Juan and Madler looked at each other in exasperation as they realized there was no way out.

Chapter 36

Commander Smith's attention to detail in planning the raid, and the precision shooting by his ETF team members, resulted in the capture of all armed men without any casualties. The wounded shooters were transported to a secure facility to receive medical attention before processing them at the police station. None of the workers had been injured during the raid. They were all arrested and taken to the station in separate cruisers so there would be no chance to agree among them on how to answer questions during their interrogation.

Borden and Cross had immediately separated Juan and Madler at the scene for the same reason and kept watch while paramedics attended to their glass cuts before escorting them to separate cruisers. For the next three hours, they joined Agent Spade of CSIS and Sergeants Crawford and Westwood of the RCMP, observing and discussing the evidence that was being collected and cataloged inside the warehouse.

The five of them arrived back at the police station just after 1:00 in the afternoon and huddled in Borden's office for a quick strategy session on how to interrogate Juan and Madler.

Borden was the first to speak, "To be honest with you, my head is still spinning on how this case has unfolded since Cross and I first headed out to the offices of Complete Real Estate five days ago. What we initially thought was a break-and-enter gone bad has turned into a web of criminal activity that stretches throughout Canada, the United States, and Mexico. Obviously, this is a massive operation that's too large to have been put together by Juan or Madler. There must be somebody higher up, from whom they take orders."

"It seems to me," offered Crawford, "that Madler is the key to understanding the identity fraud scheme that played out in British Columbia and Alberta before we caught him red-handed here. If it's okay with you, I'd like to be involved in his interrogation."

"And Juan is clearly the closest tie to the Cartel leaders we suspect have been using their funds to finance terrorist activities," added Agent Spade. "I would like the opportunity to have a crack at interrogating him."

First looking at Cross and then at Crawford and Spade, Borden replied, "I think I also speak for Detective Cross when I say that your contribution to this case so far is extremely appreciated, and we are more than happy to have you join us during interrogation. Let's start with Juan. I'll take the lead on this one. Cross, you take the lead on Madler."

The decision to interrogate Juan was personal for Borden. Ever since his son, Mark Jr., had died of an overdose, Borden had become almost obsessed with taking down drug lords. As he mentally prepared to question Juan, a drug lord in his own right, he couldn't help thinking of him as the man who might have been behind the drugs that killed his son.

As Borden and Spade walked into the interrogation room, they could see Juan was sitting with his arms folded and a disgusted look on his face, instantly signaling he would be uncooperative.

"When can I leave here? I have rights."

Borden quickly responded, "Correction Juan, you don't have rights. You're not a citizen of this country, and as to when you can leave, that won't happen for about thirty years from now if you don't answer my questions."

"How can I answer your questions when I don't know anything?" Juan asked in a half-whining voice. "My head still hurts from those flash-bangs you threw into the warehouse. Can I have something for my headache?"

"You want to talk about headache, Juan?" asked Borden. "The headache you have now is nothing compared to what's coming down the track toward you. We arrested you in a warehouse full of illegal drugs while you and a small army of armed guards were shooting at police. With all the charges you face for that, you'll be an old man by the time you ever step foot out of prison."

Agent Spade quickly jumped in, "Just to inform you, I'm with CSIS, the Canadian Security Intelligence

Service. If you don't start cooperating with us, I'll be charging you with terrorism. Just to be clear, terrorism charges will keep you behind bars forever. You will never see your family again or your friends. You will never see Mexico again and you'll die here in a Canadian prison all alone. How does that sound, Juan?"

"What are you talking about? You can't charge me with terrorism. I'm no terrorist!"

"From where I'm sitting Juan, it's pretty clear that the money you are making from selling drugs is partially being used to fund Cartel terrorist activities. We caught you with the drugs. That makes you an accessory to terrorism, wouldn't you agree detective?"

Borden knew Spade was stretching the truth, but all is fair in love and interrogation. "Absolutely. But perhaps Agent Spade won't have to charge you with terrorism if you can tell us who's really in charge of your drug smuggling and distribution operation."

"Look, you've got this all wrong. I'm not part of any drug smuggling operation. I was just at the warehouse to meet a friend when you guys came barging in. You can't prove I have anything to do with those drugs."

Now it was Borden's turn to stretch the truth. "Are you referring to your friend Madler, Juan? There's no point in continuing with this little charade. We've already talked to Madler, and he squealed like a pig. He told us all about your involvement and where you fit into this. It looks like you'll both be going away for an awfully long time."

Juan's face remained expressionless as his mind raced to consider whether Madler had thrown him under the bus. "I know you are lying to me."

Borden was instantly thankful his team had already interrogated the twelve workers arrested at the warehouse. He could make Juan think it was Madler who turned against him.

"Am I really, Juan? Then how do I know that drugs from Mexico have been coming to the warehouse for the past three months? How do I know that you arrived here just five days ago to take control of the packaging and distribution of drugs from the warehouse? How do I know that you killed a man just to make a point about who was in charge? By the way, if we ever find his body, we will add murder to the long list of charges that you already face."

"You have no proof of any of this."

Borden flipped open a file folder in front of him and turned it to show Juan the images inside. "These are wonderful pictures of your family, Juan. Nice looking kids. Because you're not a citizen, we don't have to let your family visit you while you spend the rest of your life in a Canadian prison. Your kids will only remember you from photos your wife shows them, but she'll remarry, and your pictures will probably end up in the garbage."

Spade interjected with perfect timing, "Just take a moment to let that sink in, Juan."

She and Borden had pre-planned what happened next. Each one of them would take turns asking questions in rapid succession. With a tap on Borden's foot under the table, she indicated it was his turn to start things off.

"How long have you been working for the Cartel?"

"Who do you report to?"

"Who is the brain behind this operation?"

"Who is your source of drugs in Mexico?"

"Who is your contact person in Canada?"

"How do the drugs get into Canada?"

"When is your next shipment due to arrive?"

"Are there any other warehouses across the country?"

"Answer my questions, Juan."

"Are you ready to be someone's girlfriend in prison?"

"How many people have you shot, Juan?"

"You know it's over Juan, talk to us."

"Madler will get a deal and you'll get to rot in jail."

"You will be charged with terrorism."

Juan wanted to scream. His mind was spinning.

Spade waited for a few seconds, which seemed like an eternity to Juan as the questions kept swimming around in his head. "The Cartel can't help you here Juan. You are on your own. They don't care about you and will leave you here to rot, or have you killed when you least expect an attack."

Borden hammered home Spade's comment, "We were thinking about leaking a story that you were very co-operative, and that you gave us all the names and information we needed to crush the drug trade coming from the Cartels into Canada and the US. Then we'll buy you a plane ticket and send you back to Mexico."

"You can't do that!" Juan cried out. "I'll be murdered the same day you send me back home. They will kill my family."

"Well," Borden replied. "We might not have any choice if you don't help with our investigation. It's not complicated. You help us and we'll see what we can do to keep you here and your family back home safe.

"We'll give you a new name and a new identity, and your family will even be able to move here with you when it's safe. You'll be looked after in our witness protection program after you come out of prison."

That was the cue for Sergeants Crawford and Westwood, who had been observing from behind the one-way mirror, to step into action.

Moments later, there was a deliberate knock on the interrogation room door. Borden rose from his seat and opened the door, stepping aside to make sure Juan could clearly see who was there.

"Detective Borden. I'm Sergeant Crawford of the RCMP, and I'm here with my partner Sergeant Westwood." He handed Borden a sheet of paper.

"This paper authorizes us to take custody of one Juan Estrada. Extradition papers are being prepared and we'll take custody of him now if that's not a problem. We'll both be escorting him to Mexico when the extradition papers are completed later today."

Borden took the papers from Crawford. "Can you just give us a few more minutes, Sergeant?"

"Sir, my orders are to take him now and prepare him for transport."

"I understand, but perhaps you could spare me five minutes or so?

"Yes sir, that will be fine."

"Thanks." Borden closed the door and looked at Juan. "Well Juan, unless you're willing to help us, Mexico is calling."

Juan was now visibly nervous. He stared down at the tabletop in front of him as he considered his options. Just hours ago, he was in charge, giving orders and feeling strong and secure. That wasn't the case anymore. His power was gone, and he knew it. He knew he had no future unless he made a deal with the police.

"I'll tell you what I know if you promise not to deport me and to protect my family."

"Before I make any promises, Juan, I want to hear something we can use to stop the flow of drugs into the country," replied Borden. "Let's start by you telling us who is the mastermind behind your drug smuggling operation."

Juan knew he had to be careful here not to give up Carlos Martinez and Miguel Valdez, or he would be signing a death sentence for him and his family no matter where they were. The Cartel would hunt them down and find them.

"The one thing you must understand about the Cartel is that they go to great lengths to protect the organization. It is common practice that nobody knows the person who gives them orders so that nobody can give anyone up if they are ever caught by the police. All I can tell you is that I receive instructions via burner phone from a man that has no name."

Borden couldn't hide the disappointment in his voice, "You get no points for that answer, Juan. I was hoping you would do so much better than that. The clock is still ticking on your departure for Mexico. Let's try again, shall we? How often do drugs arrive at the warehouse?"

"The drugs arrive weekly. We have a courier system of vans that pick up boxes of drugs from constantly changing locations that are sent to us via burner phone text messages."

Borden continued, "How do these drugs get into the country?"

"We cover all the bases. Hiding large shipments of drugs in transport trucks mixed in with goods that are on the shipping manifest is one way that always has and always will work. As a decoy, we place smaller shipments of drugs in rented trucks and vans that pull into customs checkpoints just ahead of the main transport. Border security gets distracted handling the confiscation of these smaller shipments while the transport trucks pass right through undetected."

Borden was not impressed. "Tell us something we don't already know Juan."

"Small Cessna airplanes are used to pick up drugs at isolated landing strips across Mexico and the United States. They drop drugs on Vancouver Island, then fly on to Victoria airport. If the aircraft is searched upon landing, the plane is clean. Once the drugs are recovered, using a GPS tracker inside the container, they are driven to the mainland from Nanaimo or the Victoria ferry terminals. Then they are transported across the country to one of our warehouses."

"How many warehouses are there?" asked Borden.

"There is one in every major Canadian city. I don't know the exact locations except for the one where you found me today."

"So far, you've covered two bases, Juan. What are the other two?"

"Some drugs are carried by people hiking in the forests and crossing into Canada in areas that are not under surveillance. The carriers have a destination map detailing where they can drop their backpacks and pick up a bag of cash, then disappear or head back and do it again."

Borden was secretly surprised at the extent of this network of smugglers. "How do the Cartels know what areas of the border don't have any security?"

"The Cartels, have a person by the name of Randy, who is constantly flying drones looking for border patrols or police activity. We have a list of all the areas we use for border crossings. Randy moves throughout these areas to make sure they are secure to cross. He is constantly on the move and has a police scanner turned on 24/7. If the police put out a call about possible drug activity, Randy immediately notifies his contacts to abort or change direction."

"How does he do that, Juan?"

"He simply sends a coded text message, so the hiker knows to head to the backup drop point."

Borden's interest was piqued, "Is Randy the only spotter they use?"

"No, there are many spotters, but they are all called Randy. We use Randy as a code name for the individuals protecting the shipments. Any alert from Randy means that one of the spotters has seen something, leading to a change in plans."

Glancing at Agent Spade, Borden nodded for her to carry on. "That's three out of four bases, Juan. Let's go for the homerun. What can you tell us that we've never heard before?"

Juan knew he was in deep now, so he might as well tell the cops everything he knew. Well, at least most things. He had to leave some things in reserve in case he needed more bargaining chips later.

"Drugs arrive by train. They are placed in thin metal containers held in place by electromagnets on the bottom of certain passenger rail cars. The box is painted the same color as the train bottom, so it goes unnoticed during any inspection.

"We have Cartel workers assigned to various railway maintenance crews across Mexico. They are responsible for placing the magnetic boxes under random passenger coaches.

"When the passenger train passes a designated drop spot en route to its destination, a cell phone is used to turn off the electromagnet, and the container falls flat between the wheels onto the tracks."

Borden interrupted, "Are those the thin metal boxes your workers were unpacking at the warehouse?"

"Yes. The train rolls away, leaving the drugs on the track in those boxes."

Spade put up her hands. "Stop, just for a second. This seems pretty far-fetched. Are you serious?"

Juan smiled. "Yes. That's the beauty of it. The Cartels are always five steps ahead of the police. Once the train is out of sight, the drugs are picked up by people waiting for the train near the side of the track. Because the train is always on time, the couriers are there for only a couple of minutes, and then gone."

Just then, there was another knock on the interrogation room door. Borden opened the door to an awaiting Sergeant Crawford. Turning to Juan, he said, "Now we're getting somewhere, Juan. I'll be back in a few minutes after I convince the RCMP to cancel your plane ticket back home."

Chapter 37

Madler was brought to the interrogation room and sat there alone, planning his strategy to mislead the police. He didn't even look up when Detective Cross and Sergeant Crawford opened the door and entered.

Cross waited until she could make direct eye contact with Madler before speaking, "Well Jason, this day hasn't gone the way you expected, has it?"

"My friends call me Madler."

"That's nice, but we're not your friends. So tell me Jason, or should we call you Jeff now? We noticed that one of the workers we arrested this morning at the warehouse was putting your picture on a passport for Jeff Sullivan."

"I have no idea what you're talking about. My name is Madler."

"Okay Madler, have it your way. I'm Detective Cross of the Toronto Police. It seems you've been a bad boy not just here, but elsewhere in Canada too. That's why you also have the pleasure of speaking with Sergeant Crawford here from the RCMP."

"I have no idea what you're referring to. When Santa Claus makes his list and checks it twice, I'm always on his 'nice' list."

"Nice people don't shoot at police, Madler. By the way, we tend to take things like that rather personally."

Madler remained silent and stared directly into the one-way mirror as if he could see Borden and Agent Spade on the other side.

Cross continued, "Why did you go straight to the warehouse after checking out of the Ford Hotel last night?"

Madler looked stunned for a moment as he realized how the police found out the location of the warehouse. "I went for a friendly game of poker with some friends."

"Funny how we didn't find a deck of playing cards anywhere at the scene. Here's what I think, Madler. You were worried that Stan and Derek Temple might rat you out, so you went to the warehouse to start working on a new identity for yourself."

"I told you I don't know anything about creating a new identity, and I don't know anyone by the name of Stan or Derek."

"Stan and Derek told us everything about your little identity theft operation. They told us how you instructed them to threaten Andrea Talbot at Complete Real Estate into giving them a thumb drive with information about all their wealthy clients. When she didn't give them the information, they broke into their office instead to steal the computers."

"I have absolutely no knowledge about that."

"Then why did we find those stolen computers, and the laptops of Carson and Chelsea Blocker that were stolen from their home, inside your warehouse on the same table where your new fake passport was being created? Tell us what you were doing with the information on those computers Madler?"

Crawford could see tiny beads of sweat appearing on Madler's forehead. He decided to turn up the pressure. "Tell us what you were planning to do with the drugs in the warehouse."

"I have nothing to do with the drugs that you found."

"That's not what the twelve workers we arrested at the scene told us, Madler. They said they've been packaging drugs there for the past three months under your direct supervision. It wasn't until five days ago that Juan Estrada showed up to take over from you."

Cross chimed in, "So we've got you and Juan as partners in crime on drug smuggling and trafficking right now. That's enough to put the two of you away for a long time. But the fact that you came out guns blazing at police officers will keep you locked up much longer. Do you want to spend the rest of your life in prison?"

"I'm growing tired of your questions. I'd like to speak with my lawyer now."

"Speaking with your lawyer is certainly within your rights, Madler, but are you sure that's a wise move?"

"What do you mean?"

"I mean, you're working for the Cartel, Madler. We'll be sure to let them know that you led us straight to a warehouse full of their product. It will take us a few days to catalog and value all the drugs we seized there during the raid, but it doesn't take a rocket scientist to calculate that the street value would have been at least $5 million.

"The last time I checked the Cartel doesn't tolerate anyone losing their money like that. You can call your lawyer and let him walk you out of the building today, but the Cartel will be waiting for that. They'll follow you wherever you go, and you'll be lucky to still be alive by the end of the day."

Cross paused to watch Madler squirm in his seat.

"Okay, detective, I can give you all the information you want, but I want a deal."

Cross looked at Crawford and then back at Madler. "If your information is credible, I will see what I can do for you. But I can't make any guarantees until I hear what you have to say."

Madler nodded in acceptance of the terms.

Cross looked straight into Madler's eyes. "Where does Juan Estrada fit into what you are doing?"

"Juan is our contact with the Mexican Cartels. He smuggles in opioids, fentanyl, cocaine, heroin, and other drugs."

"What was going on in the warehouse?" asked Crawford.

"We were re-packaging cocaine and fentanyl into smaller packages to ship across Canada."

Crawford continued, "Are there other warehouses across the country, and if so, where are they?"

Madler paused to think. There was no way he would get a deal for protection from the Cartel if he didn't give them at least some of what they wanted to know.

"There are warehouses being set up as we speak in every major city of the country. Right now, the only one that is fully operational is the one you raided today in Toronto."

"Which other cities specifically, Madler?" asked Crawford.

"Vancouver, Calgary, Winnipeg, Montreal, and Halifax."

Cross had a puzzled look on her face. "There's something I don't understand, Madler. Tell me, how did a 'nice boy' like you who steals identities get involved with drugs and the Cartel?"

"It all started rather innocently, really. They simply wanted to use me as a reliable source to provide fake identities for any of their people coming across the border into Canada.

"But once they fully understood the scope of my fraud operation, they realized my value to them as a local money machine. It costs big bucks to set up a new operation nationwide. You can't risk leasing a warehouse for Cartel activity, so you have to buy them.

"Then you need to equip them for high security. You need to build mezzanines that overlook the main floor, and you need armed guards 24/7 to patrol those mezzanines, and state-of-the-art video surveillance systems. You need to pay for an infrastructure of couriers to both deliver and distribute the drugs from each warehouse. We're talking millions of dollars in investment.

"Trying to get that much money into the country from Mexico would have left too much of a paper trail for the authorities to follow. So, they wanted to use my expertise to bankroll their start-up."

Crawford's curiosity was piqued. "How exactly did that work?"

"The personal information on wealthy people we acquired from the real estate offices was used to steal property titles and re-finance the mortgage for much higher than the original value. To avoid suspicion, we always re-mortgaged to just under the maximum allowed. We told the banks we were re-mortgaging to fund major renovations.

"The banks loved this because not only would they make money on the mortgages, but also when the house value increased. A higher house value helped the bank if they needed to invoke a Power of Sale on the property. We ran this scam when the owner was away on business or traveling for pleasure.

"But that wasn't the only way we raised quick cash. The file of each wealthy client gave us everything we needed to create fake identities that matched the owners of expensive real estate. Any time a snowbird would head south for the winter to Florida for six months, we created counterfeit identities for them using the faces of our con artists. Then we went to local real estate companies to list their properties for sale.

"When the sale went through, we pocketed the money from the purchase directly, without the real homeowners ever knowing what was going on. When they returned from Florida, they would find the new owners occupying their home. Millions of dollars can be made in a single month using this tactic. It's like shooting fish in a barrel."

Madler wasn't sure how much more he should tell the cops at this point, but he knew he had to give them something big for them to act on now.

"Here's one more thing you might want to know. Next week, the Cartel is going to make the biggest drug drop yet. Everything up until now has been a test run to iron out the bugs. All I know is that the shipment is coming into the country by rail, but I'm not sure what day all this is happening."

Cross was now sitting on the edge of her seat. "Tell us everything you know about this Madler, and we'll do what we can to protect you from the Cartel."

"This is why Juan is here now. He was getting everything in place to fully ramp up the operation so the drugs can be received, processed, and moved across Canada. I have told you everything I know. That's it."

"You haven't told us everything, Madler. You still haven't told us who you are working for. Who recruited you to help the Cartel get started with their new operations here?"

Madler paused to think. If he spilled the beans on this, he would surely be a dead man walking. "Before I answer that, I need to know we have a deal. I need to know that you can protect me from the Cartel."

Cross looked at Crawford for agreement, then turned to make eye contact with Madler. "You have our word. What can you tell us?"

"His name is Carlos Martinez. He runs the entire Cartel operation in Canada from Ottawa. I met him there over a nice dinner in his favorite restaurant. Since then, we have only ever communicated via burner phone."

Upon hearing the name, Borden, who was still watching behind the one-way mirror along with Danielle Spade, did a quick Google search for 'Carlos Martinez Ottawa.' The result that popped up stunned them both.

Moments later, there was a knock at the interrogation room door. A uniformed officer was standing outside when Cross opened the door. "Excuse me, detective, but Detective Borden wants to speak with you. He said it is urgent."

As Cross stepped into the hallway, she saw Borden waiting for her a few feet away. He handed her the digital tablet he had used for the Google search. "Show this to Madler."

Returning to the interrogation room, she first showed the image on the tablet to Sergeant Crawford and then put it on the table in front of Madler.

"Is this the man you had dinner with in Ottawa?"

"Yes, that's him," confirmed Madler. "Mexico's ambassador to Canada."

Chapter 38

Chelsea smiled as she watched Carson gently patting the horse and speaking softly into its ear. The horse just stood there resting its head on Carson's good shoulder. It was as though two friends were having a quiet moment together. Carson knew that the horse didn't have a clue what he was talking about, but Chelsea knew, and she loved the soothing voice she heard as Carson spoke.

He was talking about how much he missed this place and how happy he was to be home again. Ever since the shooting, he had become a very different man than the one she was so close to divorcing. Not once had he checked his cell phone for messages from the office since they arrived here two days ago. He was fully present in each moment and mindful of everything and everyone around him. And, for the first time in as long as she could remember, he made her feel both seen and heard.

"Chelsea, let's saddle up a couple of these horses and head out to do a little exploring around the ranch. I have no idea what it looks like beyond the house and the barn here. After Luke and Melissa got married and bought this place, I was always working so hard at my dad's ranch that I never had time to see the whole property. Luke says there are 650 acres for us to go find a perfect spot for that picnic lunch Melissa made for us."

After about 20 minutes of riding, they came to a fast-running stream that had swollen its normal size and overflowed its banks with the deluge of water that fell during the storm a few days ago.

Soon the stream and rolling hills gave way to a forested area where they followed the grass and dirt path to a higher pasture that gave them a panoramic view of the entire ranch and the surrounding areas. They could see all around them how the countryside was formed by glaciers during the last ice age. The mountains stood tall in the distance as they watched Luke's cattle roaming in the fields below them, munching on grass and paying no attention to anything.

"Chelsea, can you hear that?"

"Hear what Carson?"

"Just listen. Can you hear the breeze?"

Chelsea nodded slowly, "Yes. I can hear it. It's like a calming whisper."

"Now, look up to the sky for a minute. What do you feel?"

Tilting her head back, Chelsea sat in silence atop her horse and closed her eyes. After a moment, she smiled broadly. "I feel the warmth of the sun's rays on my face. It feels like it's melting away all my stress and fears. I've never felt like this living in Toronto, Carson."

"I never have either, Chelsea. The city is a concrete jungle where everyone's living in non-stop hustle and bustle. There's no feeling of peace and calm like this to be had in a place like that. So, why are we living in Toronto? Why don't we move back here so we can feel this peace and calm every day?"

"Carson, I haven't seen you this happy in a long time. If living here is what makes you happy, then it makes me happy too. Let's do it!"

Deciding that this was the perfect spot for their picnic, Carson and Chelsea dismounted and tied the horses to a nearby tree. Almost two hours passed as they enjoyed their lunch and talked about how and when they could move back to Canmore.

After packing up their picnic gear and feeding the horses a treat of carrot sticks, they rode along the perimeter of the hilltop to get a 360-degree view of Luke's ranch.

"Look back there, Carson. We are so high up and so far away that the ranch house looks more like a doll's house."

"It does," chuckled Carson, "You're absolutely right."

"And look at the pond down there nestled so nicely between that hill and that little patch of pasture before the trees."

Looking at what Chelsea had just described, Carson saw something else. "You know what I see there? I see a tee box on top of that hill, with a 200-yard carry to a golf green on the other side of the pond. It would make a perfect par 3 hole."

Pointing a little further left, Carson exclaimed, "And look over there, Chelsea! Beside that green is another perfect tee box with a dog-leg fairway running alongside the treeline. Luke's property is the perfect place for a golf course!".

Hardly able to contain his excitement, Carson took pictures with his cell phone of every view from the top of the hill before he and Chelsea rode back to the barn.

After heading inside and freshening up, they sat with Luke and Melissa to enjoy a cup of tea. The mid-afternoon tea break was something Melissa started soon after she and Luke were married. It was a perfect way for Luke to relax after finishing his chores around the ranch and for Melissa to enjoy some quality time with him.

Looking over at Luke and Melissa, Carson could hardly contain his excitement. "Chelsea and I have some news we can't wait to share with you. We've decided to move back here to Canmore as soon as we can sell our home in Toronto. Coming back here has made me realize just how much I've missed this place. And a magic moment happened out there today that makes me think this is what we're supposed to do."

"That's wonderful news little brother. We've missed not having you around here, and I know Mom and Dad will be delighted too. But what's this magic moment you mentioned?"

"While we were admiring how gorgeous everything looked from the highest point on the property, I had an epiphany of sorts. Chelsea and I talked about it on the ride back, and she thinks it's a great idea, assuming that you and Melissa both agree too."

Melissa was bursting with curiosity. "Agree to what?"

"Luke, you told me that running the ranch has been hard on you, and that it's been a struggle to make ends meet. The roof needs fixing, and some of the fences need mending, but it's a daily struggle for you and Melissa, isn't it?"

"I hate to admit it Carson, but some days I wonder how much longer we can keep the ranch going. Just last month, Melissa and I were talking about listing the property for sale."

"Well, I'm glad you didn't list it, because you're sitting on a gold mine. This property is perfect for a PGA Championship Golf Course. The natural mounding provides the perfect vantage point for huge galleries of fans to watch the tour pros play a sponsored event. Here, just look at these pictures I took on my phone."

Luke and Melissa listened in amazement as Carson scrolled through each picture and explained his future vision for their property.

"A championship golf course would require about 350 acres including the clubhouse, parking, and practice range. That would still leave you with about 300 acres to continue ranching. The golf course would supplement your income and provide for a handsome retirement for you and Melissa someday."

"That's great Carson, but I can't manage a golf course and the ranch. I can barely keep up with the ranch as it is. And I don't know the first thing about building and running a golf course!"

"That's no problem. I've thought about that as well. Doug and I have always dreamed of opening a championship PGA golf course. We thought we'd never be able to make that dream come true because we didn't have the money or the land to make it work. But you and Melissa have the land. That's your investment in this little venture.

"Doug and I have the money to finance the building of the course and the clubhouse. Doug was right when he said there was money to be made in Toronto real estate. And over the past ten years, he and I have made a small fortune buying, selling, and renting properties.

"And think about this too. As we become established, we could take your remaining property and turn it into a destination dude ranch. Guests would supply the labor and muck out the stalls, round up the cattle, mend fences, and feed the livestock. They would be paying us to have the full experience of what it's like living and working a real Alberta ranch."

Luke's face had the most incredulous look, "Oh my goodness Carson, are you for real?"

"Yes, and Doug and I could finance a small hotel with a dining room here on the property where people could rent rooms while having their dude ranch experience. So we'd make money from the hospitality services, the dude ranch, and the golf course. And once the course grows in and matures, we can broker a deal with the PGA tour to host a tournament here. That's why this property is a gold mine! I'm proposing that you, me, and Doug go into this as equal partners."

"That sounds good to me. But how do you know that Doug will agree to all this Carson?"

Carson grinned from ear to ear as he reached to pick up his cell phone. He punched the pre-programmed number for Doug.

"Hey, Carson. Perfect timing. I was just about to call you with some good news. I just finished closing your deal with William and Sara Porter. They bought a nice little hobby farm north of the city for just under $5 million. You made a nice chunk of change in commission."

"That is great news, Doug. But I didn't call to get an update on my outstanding deals. Remember the promise you made the other day? I picked up the phone to tell you it's time to come home."

Chapter 39

As Carlos Martinez stepped into the parking garage of the Mexican embassy in Ottawa, his security detail and driver were waiting beside his Mercedes. He was on his way to an important luncheon date.

Looking at his cell phone as it began ringing, he recognized the number and remotely slid the glass wall to isolate and soundproof himself in the back seat of the vehicle.

"Mr. President. We are secure in my vehicle. What can I do for you?"

"You can tell me what the hell is going on with this drug raid in Toronto three days ago. Did you know about this?"

"No, I had no advanced knowledge of the raid or I would have intervened."

"What do you mean you would have intervened?"

"Well, I would've warned our people and moved our product from the warehouse to minimize our exposure and loss. The police would have found nothing and considered the operation a complete failure given the manpower they wasted."

"The Canadian government is officially asking for me to remove you as ambassador and revoke your diplomatic status so they can press charges against you."

"Charges for what, Mr. President? I was visited at the embassy by two RCMP officers and a CSIS Agent yesterday. Their claims that I am somehow in control of a huge drug smuggling and distribution operation within Canada are purely hearsay. They have no proof. You will simply tell the Canadian government that this is an obvious smear tactic against the Mexican government."

"This situation is unacceptable! How could you let this happen? I don't like being put in this position."

"Well, Mr. President, I don't like it any more than you do. But perhaps I should remind you that you wouldn't have your job if my colleagues and I hadn't funded your campaign, placing you in a position to be elected as President."

"What are you saying, Martinez?"

"We control the Mexican government and can place anybody in any position we choose. You answer to us. We do not answer to you."

"Go to hell Ambassador!"

"No, you will do exactly what we tell you to, and you won't threaten us ever if you want to keep your job. You work for me. Got that?"

"The hell I do. I work for Mexico, and I work for the people of my country."

"Mr. President, if you ever want to see your wife again, and your children grow up, and your parents grow old, it would be wise for you to do exactly what we tell you to do, or they will all disappear."

"Is that a threat Mr. Ambassador?"

"No, it's a promise, Mr. President."

As the car rolled to a stop in front of the restaurant, Martinez abruptly terminated the call and hurried inside.

A young woman with long, wavy black hair looked up at him with piercing brown eyes as he strode toward the table, trying unsuccessfully to hide his exasperation. "Good afternoon, Mr. Ambassador. Is everything all right?".

"No, I just got off the phone with the old lady who calls himself the President of our country. He is such a weakling."

"Do you want me to handle that for you, sir?"

"There may be a time and a place for that later."

"I would very much enjoy resolving that issue for you."

"Thank you, Tina. I'm sure you would. But you have a more pressing issue to resolve right now. Do you have everything you need to make this happen?"

A smile came slowly to Tina's face. "Yes, I do. They'll never see it coming. They'll never know what hit them."

Chapter 40

Borden hung up the phone and looked across his desk at Cross. "That was the Chief. He said there is nothing more that we can do. The Ambassador has diplomatic immunity, and the Mexican government is refusing to recall him. We can't arrest Carlos Martinez as long as he remains an ambassador. It doesn't matter how many laws he breaks. We can't touch him. The RCMP and CSIS are also off the case."

Cross shook her head slowly in disbelief. "We've come all this way. We got justice for Carson Blocker, Bob Jackson, and Andrea Talbot. But, if we don't take Martinez down, nothing changes. The drugs we seized in the raid won't mean a thing. The Cartel will have another warehouse full of them in no time."

"And more kids will die like my son did. I can't let that happen on my watch, Cross. This isn't over. We're not finished chasing after justice."

***

Borden and Cross will return.